MW00614381

NO SAFE
HAVEN

A LAST SANCTUARY NOVEL

KYLA STONE

NO SAFE HAVEN

A LAST SANCTUARY NOVEL

KYLA STONE

PAPER MOON PRESS

No Safe Haven

Copyright © 2018 by Kyla Stone All rights reserved. This book or any portion thereof may not be reproduced or used in any manner whatsoever without the express written permission of the publisher except for the use of brief quotations in a book review.

This book is a work of fiction. Any references to historical events, real people, or real places are used fictitiously. Other names, characters, places, and events are products of the author's imagination, and any resemblances to actual events or places or persons, living or dead, is entirely coincidental.

Printed in the United States of America

Cover design by Deranged Doctor Designs

Book formatting by Vellum

First Printed in 2018

ISBN 978-1-945410-22-2

Paper Moon Press

Atlanta, Georgia

www.PaperMoonPress.com

 Created with Vellum

ALSO BY KYLA STONE

Beneath the Skin

Before You Break

Real Solutions for Adult Acne

Rising Storm

Falling Stars

Burning Skies

Breaking World

Raging Light

No Safe Haven

1

S ilence could drown a person.

At least, that's what Raven Nakamura's mother had said three years ago—the day she left for good.

Her mom wasn't quite right, though. It wasn't silence. There were more sounds than Raven could count—the whirring of insects, the breeze rustling the elm and maple trees lining the flagstone paths, and the constant calls, screeches, hoots, bellows, grunts, and growls of the numerous and varied exotic animals that lived here.

Maybe it was isolation that could drown a person.

More likely, her mom was simply full of crap, telling herself whatever would justify leaving her daughter behind.

Raven watched the swishing tail of the Siberian tiger lying twenty feet below her. He blinked at her, yellow eyes shining with a vicious, uncanny intelligence. A seven-year-old male, Vlad weighed over five hundred pounds, and stretched nine feet from nose to tail.

He was a creature of incredible power and beauty. Rippling orange fur striped with luscious inky black. A majestic head with a thick white ruff. Sharp fangs glinting from impressive jaws. Enormous paws that could rip a man's face off. Every inch of him was formidable—and exquisitely lethal.

The tiger was just fine with isolation. They were solitary creatures by nature, nomads of the jungle. Or, in this case, of Haven Wildlife Refuge, the family zoo Raven's father owned and operated in the rolling hills of northern Georgia.

Raven wasn't afraid of being alone. She vastly preferred it to human contact of any kind. She'd gotten that from her father. It was her mother who couldn't stand the loneliness, who hated it so much she preferred to leave her daughter behind and seek companionship elsewhere than stay.

Raven gritted her teeth. Usually, she was successful at keeping thoughts of her mother buried in a dark corner of her brain, shoved somewhere down deep. Out of sight, out of mind.

Except for today. October sixteen. Raven's eighteenth birthday.

Ironically, the only person who'd remembered was the one who'd chosen to leave. Also ironic; her scatter-brained, over-emotional, depressed mother had managed to send the package three weeks early—which was fortunate, since the postal service hadn't delivered the mail for nineteen days.

Scraps of clouds drifted across the sun, shining brilliantly in the cobalt sky. It was sixty-five degrees. She was dressed in her usual cargo pants, black work boots, and a loose T-shirt. Her mask hung loose around her neck, just in case.

It was a beautiful fall day—too beautiful for the dark tangle of emotions knotted inside her.

She held the small unopened box in both hands. She didn't want to know what it was. She considered chucking it into the tiger enclosure so Vlad could rip it to shreds as part of his daily enrichment activities.

But if she threw it away unopened and unread, the little niggle of curiosity tugging at her would remain unassuaged. This was the last birthday she'd ever have here, which meant this was likely the last present from her mother she'd ever receive.

Raven shifted on the tiger house's roof, leaning over the edge to catch a glimpse of her hiking backpack slumped against the steel wall. She'd spent the last week packing, stealthily scrounging supplies: snare wire for small animal traps, single person tent and sleeping bag, life straw and water filtration tablets, a tin cup, plate, and pan, flint and spare lighter, compass, toiletries, hunting knife, granola bars, and a few self-heating meal pouches.

She'd packed in secret, but she needn't have worried. Her father noticed nothing unless it had to do with the exotic animals or the maintenance of the refuge. He barely noticed her unless he was instructing her in one of his favorite subjects: survival skills, hunting and zoology, or how best to scrub black bear urine out of concrete.

And now, with the keepers failing to show for the third week in a row, her father was pulling sixteen-hour-a day shifts just to keep it all running. She was right there with him, working until her fingers blistered, until her bones ached with exhaustion. But to him, it was like she didn't even exist.

She ignored the pang between her ribs. It was just as well.

Today she was leaving.

She'd had enough. Enough of people that only hurt her. Enough of this place that once seemed fascinating and magical but now only held dark memories of disappointment and regret.

She knew how to survive on her own. Knew what berries were poisonous, which plants and nuts and mushrooms were edible, how to track game and set snares, how to construct a shelter in the rain, or start a fire a dozen different ways.

Her family owned a hunting cabin fifty miles away. It was deep in the woods, far from humans, far from the chaos gripping the over-crowded cities. Most importantly, far from her dad and the sharp, bitter memories of her mother.

A person could be loneliest around other people. Living, work-ing, and breathing right next to someone else—a stranger who shouldn't have been that distant.

A loneliness that hurt more than actually being alone. Maybe her mother had been talking about *that*.

It was time to go, to strike out on her own.

No matter how much she wanted to, she couldn't leave the gift unopened. She despised herself for her weakness, but she couldn't stop herself.

Raven set aside the attached letter and slid her fingernails between the cardboard flaps of the box, slicing through the tape. She dug through the balls of Styrofoam and pulled out a small knife.

The handle was off-white, a polymer imitation of ivory, and carved in the shape of a howling wolf. The blade was short, slightly curved, and sharp. It was a whittling knife for the animals Raven used to carve and display on her bedroom windowsill.

She hadn't carved anything in three years. Not since the day her mother left.

Raven sighed, disappointed in spite of herself. What had she expected? Last year, her mother had sent a ridiculous hoverboard—as if she'd forgotten Raven wasn't ten anymore. The year before that, an old, preowned SmartFlex, which was useless, because she already had one—just as old, just as preowned, and stuffed in a drawer.

Her mother didn't know her anymore.

She flicked the blade closed and shoved the whittling knife into her pocket. She didn't want it, but she couldn't leave it on top of the tiger house. A strong wind might blow it into the enclosure, and Vlad, who ate everything, would swallow it whole.

Her gaze landed on the white square of the envelope. Only her mother actually wrote letters instead of messaging. But then, the internet had gone sketchy weeks ago. Nothing was working anymore. Maybe her mother was smarter than Raven was giving her credit for.

Her stomach tightened. She didn't want to read it. What was the point? It would only make her feel like crap.

Almost against her will, her fingers crept toward it. Giving in, she grabbed the letter, ripped it open, and skimmed her mom's familiar precise, flowing script with eyes that had suddenly grown traitorously blurry.

There were the usual miss-yous and love-yous, each one like a stab to Raven's gut. A few lines toward the end caught her eye. *I'm coming to get you,* her mom had written. *With everything that's happened, it's too dangerous for you there.*

Her heart lurched in her chest. She fumbled for the envelope and rechecked the date stamped on the front. Almost three weeks ago. Her mom said she was coming. For the first time in three years.

So where was she?

I've messaged your father so many times, but the connection here has been spotty this last week. I don't know how long it will last. Hopefully, you have been sheltered from most of it, but things are bad. Everything is falling apart out there. I'm worried this is it. The end.

The Settlement is a safe place for us. There are good people here, and it is well-fortified. Until I come, wear your mask. Be careful. If, for some reason, I'm prevented from reaching you, then come here. Find good people you can trust. Whatever you do, don't be alone.

I love you.

Raven balled the letter in her fist and crumpled it between her fingers. Her hands trembled, her knuckles whitening. Had her mother really found a safe place? Was she really going to leave it to come for Raven?

Raven clenched her jaw. Old pain sprouted in her gut, tangling her stomach in knots. What did her mom know? She thought she could ride in on a white horse and save everyone, yet she hadn't even bothered to visit in all this time. She was the one who'd run off—who was she to decide to care now?

No thanks. Raven could handle things just fine on her own. She'd been taking care of herself for years—since long before her mother had left. Aiko Nakamura had abandoned her daughter long ago, seeking something she'd never been able to find.

Still, despite her anger and resentment, Raven's breath quickened as she stared at the letter. If her mom had really tried to come, she hadn't made it. Had something happened to her? Raven knew the commune where her mother had found refuge was near Elijay in the north mountains of Georgia. It was dangerous for a woman to travel alone in the best of times, especially through gang-controlled Atlanta.

But now?

There were a hundred things that could have gone wrong, a hundred threats—from the roving gangs of thugs and killers, the hungry, desperate people driven to steal, or worse, the millions of coughing, feverish infected spreading the virus.

Raven tried to tell herself she didn't care, that it didn't matter. But of course, it did. Her mother was still her mother, no matter how thick and bitter the distance between them.

A frantic shout splintered the air.

Raven jerked her head up, stiffening. She wasn't supposed to be on the tiger house roof—ever—and if her father saw her hiking backpack...but no, it was the head zookeeper, Zachariah Harris. He was stumbling along the path at the top of the hill near the bobcat enclosure.

Raven hadn't seen him in days, not since he first started coughing. Her father had insisted he quarantine himself, holing up in his loft above the Grizzly Grill, the park's restaurant.

Wearing her N95 respiratory mask and plastic gloves, she'd tried to bring him food and water, but Zachariah had locked the door and shooed her away. "Your father would kill me," he'd said with a grunt and a pained laugh that swiftly dissolved into a phlegmy, wracking coughing fit.

What was Zachariah doing? Why had he left his room? Was it possible he was getting better?

If he had the virus, it was unlikely, based on the vlogger reports inundating the newsfeeds the last several weeks. The same hope she'd clung to all week flared through her—maybe it wasn't the infection. Maybe he'd only contracted the flu.

She took a steeling breath, slipped to the edge of the roof, crouched, and leapt to the ground. It was a long drop, but she softened her legs and curled into a roll before scrambling to her feet, brushing off twigs, pine needles, and mulch.

She whistled one long note, two short ones—Vlad's signal for food.

Behind the tiger house, in an area off-limits to visitors, she could get right up to the eighteen-foot fence. The rest of the enclosure was circled by a deep ditch surrounding a perimeter wall that was six feet high on the tiger's side, but only four feet high on the visitors' side, giving the illusion of close, unobscured proximity.

Vlad usually lounged on a rock shelf beside his shallow bathing pool, a waterfall streaming above him. The rocks were a polymer replica airbrushed to look authentically aged and weathered; the waterfall poured from a hidden PVC pipe.

Vlad sauntered over and eyed her, ears pricked, waiting impatiently. She pulled a piece of dried venison from her cargo pocket. Normally, tigers only ate raw meat, but Vlad had developed a taste for jerky. She took several steps back and hurled it over the fence. Vlad's head snapped toward it. He pounced and inhaled the venison in a blink.

Vlad prowled back to the fence and pressed his enormous body against it, chuffing eagerly for a good petting like some hugely overgrown house cat. Tigers didn't purr when they were happy or content; they chuffed, which sounded like a cough.

Carefully, on full alert, she pushed her fingers between the chain-link and scratched his thick fur along his flank, far from his dangerous jaws. He chuffed encouragingly as she felt the solid bulk of him, his muscles taut as cables beneath the lush softness of his fur.

No matter how tame he acted, she could never let her guard down—not for a fraction of a second. Vlad was a magnificent creature; he was also a voracious, powerful, and efficient predator. Once, she'd seen him take down a hawk in mid-flight a full twelve feet off the ground.

And this particular tiger had an appetite for his human keepers. At his last home, Vlad's uber-rich owner would parade him before his aristocratic, elite friends on a gold chain during decadent parties —until the tiger attacked two people, killing one and horribly maiming the other in the time it took for a security guard to raise his tranquilizer gun and dart him.

Maybe that's what they deserved for forcing an obstinate tiger to socialize. More likely, they'd taunted and abused him to the point of desperation, until he finally struck back.

She withdrew her hand. The tiger turned his great head, ears flicking, and gave her a lazy stare, as if affronted.

"Don't look at me like that," she muttered.

Another yell drew her attention. Zachariah was closer now, staggering toward her. There was something...off about him, something *wrong* in the jerky way he moved, in the ashen pallor of his face.

Instinctively, she took a step back. She pulled the mask hanging around her neck up over her nose and mouth. She cursed herself for leaving her gloves in her room.

"Zachariah," she said. "I thought you were sick. I thought—" Her voice broke off, her throat closing like a fist.

The Zachariah she knew was a spry and cheerful black man in his sixties, his skin the color of rich, damp earth, his face scored with deep wrinkles, his eyes always sparkling with humor. Zachariah had worked at Haven as head zookeeper for fifteen years, as much a fixture as Vlad or Electra, the park's elderly, arthritic bobcat.

This Zachariah was something different.

His bloodshot eyes bulged, the veins bursting until his entire eyeball glistened crimson. Blood was smeared below both of his eyes and around his gaping mouth. His skin was gray, his face both simultaneously gaunt and bloated.

Red-specked foam glistened at the corners of his mouth. A fetid stench emanated from him, one with which she was well-acquainted from living among carnivores—the rancid odor of rot, of decomposing, maggot-riddled flesh.

Raven took another step back. A small part of her registered that she was too near the fence, but the horror crashing through her blotted everything else out.

She swallowed the acid rising in the back of her throat. "Zachariah, you should lie down—"

Zachariah didn't seem to hear her. He lunged at Raven, seizing her arms with an impossibly iron grip.

Behind her, Vlad gave a tense, uneasy growl.

"Help me!" Zachariah screamed, only inches from her face. Blood-flecked spittle struck her cheeks, landed on her eyelashes.

His hands were burning on her bare arms. His whole body radiated a terrible heat. She tried to jerk away, but he was strong, impossibly strong. "Let go!"

"Save me!" he shrieked.

Terror spiked through her. The mask was a flimsy thing, useless this close. If a single microscopic droplet entered her system through her mouth, nose, eyes, or ears—she knew what would happen. She'd watched the newsfeeds reporting the overrun hospitals, the millions of sick—then billions, all dying and dead.

Zachariah coughed again, splattering phlegm onto her face. His cheeks were hollowed, spidered with swollen, pulsing, purple-black veins.

Behind her, Vlad was working himself into a frenzy. He slammed against the fence, letting out a savage, rumbling growl.

"Back away!"

She looked up, still half-frozen in shock. Her dad was running up the path from the direction of the lodge and the park entrance.

He waved his arms wildly. "Get away from him!"

Finally, Raven wrenched her arm free. She stumbled back, her spine striking the fence for an instant—Vlad snarling, hurling himself at the chain-link—before she regained her senses and staggered away.

Vlad's massive claws scraped against metal inches from where her head had just been, the fence shuddering from his considerable weight. The tiger wasn't focused on her—his piercing yellow gaze swung between her father and Zachariah, his ears flattened, tail lashing.

Raven leaned against the wall of the tiger house, gasping for breath. "Dad."

Her father stood between her and Zachariah, a tranquilizer gun gripped in both hands. He pointed the gun at Zachariah, the man he'd worked with every day for over a decade. His expression was taut, his eyes blazing. "He has it, Raven. He has the Hydra virus."

2

"**G**o home, Zachariah," Raven's father ordered, steel in his voice. He spoke calmly, but the tranquilizer gun pointed at Zachariah's chest told a different story. "You don't belong out here."

Zachariah blinked at him with eyes red as blood. "You have to help me!"

"Go home right now."

Raven tensed, unsure what her dad was prepared to do if Zachariah defied him, if he came at them again. He was delirious, too sick to understand what he was doing, to recognize his own aggression.

On her left, Vlad paced and snarled at the fence line, lips pulled all the way back from his gleaming fangs. He reared onto his hind legs, growling, and lunged against the fence again and again. Vlad despised guns—the sight of one always worked him into a furious frenzy—but Zachariah's sickly odor and bizarre, jerky movements were unhinging him. She felt as unsettled as he did.

She stared at Zachariah in growing horror. He was barely recognizable as Zachariah, let alone a human. But his eyes, even reddened and rimmed in blood, were filled with an all-too-human emotion —terror.

"Please," she whispered, her gut churning with dread, with that twisted, palpable sense of *wrongness*. "You're hurting yourself. Please go home so you can rest."

"Home," Zachariah mumbled. He shook his head violently, as if he were shaking off fleas or gnats. He took a step back, then another. Raven's father tracked him with the tranq gun.

The zookeeper coughed again, a harsh, retching sound. "I have to go...I have to..."

He never finished his thought. His gaze roamed, disjointed, jittery and frenetic, then with sudden focus, fixed upon Raven. He blinked rapidly. For an instant, he was lucid. He *saw* her. "I'm sorry," he whispered, throat gurgling. "I didn't mean to—I didn't want to...I'm so sorry."

"Zachariah—"

He lurched away, staggering up the path toward the foxes, the zebra, and the bobcat, in the opposite direction of the restaurant and his loft.

Neither Raven nor her father stopped him. She was just relieved that he was gone for the moment, that the threat was past. Except it wasn't. Heart still thudding in her throat, she tentatively touched her face. Her fingers came away wet with speckled phlegm and blood.

"He coughed on you," her father said in a low, rough voice. "Did it get in your eyes or mouth?"

Her pulse roared in her ears. "I—I don't know."

"Don't touch anything." He dug into his pocket, tugged out a spare pair of plastic gloves and a bottle of disinfectant spray, and tossed them to her. "Take off the mask."

She pulled on the gloves. Carefully, she unhooked her blood-tinged mask and threw it on the ground. She'd take care of it later, but now, she just wanted it off.

She sprayed her face and hands with the disinfectant spray and scrubbed her skin until it felt raw. It wouldn't do anything, not if the virus was already inside her, but she did it anyway. She had to do *something*. She carefully peeled off the gloves and dropped them beside the mask.

She offered her father the disinfectant spray, but he just shook his head. "Keep it."

She stuffed it into her pocket, her fingers trembling, her skin crawling, every hair on the back of her neck standing on end.

Listening to the statistics and watching talking heads repeat the staggering, mind-numbing numbers hadn't seemed real. Neither had the vids of the rioting outside government buildings and soldiers with guns at checkpoints, enforcing curfews in cities she'd never been to. Not even the disappearing staff had made it real.

First it was the bat-flu, a terrible epidemic in itself. Millions of people complaining of headaches, coughing fits, chills and fevers. Then another illness cropped up, flawlessly imitating a simple cold and then the flu. It spread like wildfire. People continued to go to work, to school, to stores and restaurants and airports. By the time health officials began reporting hemorrhaging from eyes, mouths, and ears, it was too late. The virus had spread too rapidly. There was no way to contain it.

Over four weeks ago, the president had died from the Hydra virus. The newly sworn-in President, Amanda Sloane, had given an explosive presidential address, announcing the pandemic was an engineered virus, a bioweapon released by terrorists, designed to be highly contagious and highly virulent. The president had declared martial law, promising to eradicate the virus and restore order.

She'd failed. Rumors spread that the surviving government had fled to some underground bunker, abandoning the country to the ravages of the virus and the desperation of those that survived.

After the president's address, Raven's father immediately closed the refuge and locked the gates, though by then, the visitors had already slowed to a trickle. One by one, the staff had called in sick or simply stopped showing up. Hakeem, the bird and reptile keeper, and Sonya, the big cat keeper, had been out for five weeks. Raj, who cared for the bears and the wolves, hadn't been heard from in a month.

At first, rolling power outages lasted for hours or days at a time. News coverage was sporadic at best. The vloggers reported the millions dead, then billions. The newsfeeds began to repeat old information, the same reports and health warnings replaying over and over. Then the net went black altogether. The power followed.

Luckily, Haven had back-up generators. Zachariah had scavenged up plenty of gas in those early days, though it was currently running low.

But power was one of the least of their problems now.

Her father stared at her, jaw working, silent and angry. "How could you be so careless?"

She flinched. "I had my mask."

"But no gloves." There was blame in his voice, recrimination. "You didn't run from him. You let him walk right up to you."

She went rigid. He was right. She'd allowed her thoughts to be consumed by other things—her plans for escape, her mother—and she hadn't been alert. She'd let her guard down. "It was—he's Zachariah!"

"It doesn't matter," her father said, his voice hard. "You don't put yourself in danger for anyone. Do you understand me?"

"Yes." She forced herself to think of something other than the microscopic virus particles that could be percolating through her blood in that very moment. "Zachariah is suffering. He needs medicine."

Her father lowered the tranq gun and shook his head. His long black hair was threaded with gray and tied in a knot at the back of his neck. He was trim and lanky, with hard, wiry muscles from years of heavy labor. His face was lean and weathered. She couldn't see his mouth beneath his mask, but she knew it was pressed into a grim slash.

"No." He rubbed sweat from his forehead with the back of his arm. His skin was sallow. Bruises circled his eyes from weeks of stress and little sleep.

He turned away from her, likely to head to the rear of the park, to the wolves, were he spent his free time after all the animals had been fed and cared for. Her father was a man of few words. Her mother had hated it. Raven had grown used to it, resigned to reality. But today, his reticence was unacceptable.

"No? What do you mean, no?" She repeated the same thing she'd said eight days ago, when Zachariah first started coughing and he'd quarantined himself inside his loft. "There must be something we can do. Call Dr. El-Hashem in town—"

"No doctors left to call," her father said, his accent thickening. He'd moved to the states from Tokyo when he was a kid. He barely had an accent unless he was angry or upset.

Her mind filled with the newsfeed images of the overrun hospitals and medical centers, guarded by soldiers refusing the sick at gunpoint. The screaming children, the desperate, weeping parents.

"What about Dr. Carter?" she said, even as she knew it was hopeless.

Dr. Carter, the exotic animal vet who doctored all the parks' animals, hadn't come to take care of one of the timber wolves' abscess three weeks ago. On vet visit days, he'd always let her assist with the fecal screening programs, routine vaccinations, and other issues that cropped up. Kodiak, a two-hundred-and-sixty-pound black bear, needed a claw cutting for an ingrown toenail; Gizmo, a bonobo, suffered a toothache that required an extraction under anesthesia.

Her dad had her message Dr. Carter again and again. Finally, the vet's wife had answered, coughing and raw with grief; he was dead, another casualty of the Hydra virus.

"Then the pharmacy in town—"

Her dad whirled on her. His eyes, black as onyx and mirrors of her own, burned with some inner heat. "Too dangerous."

Fear stuck in her throat like a hook. "Zachariah is our friend. He's worked here for forever. He stayed to help even after everything went to hell. We can't just—"

"He's dying anyway," her father said flatly, his fingers tightening on the tranq gun.

"I know." She gestured helplessly. "He's also suffering. He's in pain. There are meds—"

"I said no."

Her dad coughed into his mask. He had asthma—he was always coughing. The stress—and the mask—made it worse. A bead of sweat rolled down the side of his face. Vlad continued to snarl his discontent, hurling himself at the fence. He wouldn't stop until her father put away his gun. But he didn't put it away, even though Vlad was clearly agitated. Deeper in the park, several of the wolves started to howl.

The breeze rustled through the trees, all rich shades of fiery red and burnt orange and plum purple, the pathways underfoot littered with fallen leaves. Dread settled into her stomach like a block of ice. "You want to just leave him? Let him suffer?"

"How do you think he got infected? He went into town for more gas and to get meat from the renderer. I warned him to be careful. He wasn't careful enough." He winced, like speaking the words pained him. "You will not risk yourself for him, for anyone."

She gave a sharp, frustrated jerk of her head, capitulating the same way she had before—the same way she always did. It made her hate herself. It made her want to grab her pack and run as far away from this place as she could.

Her dad coughed again into the crook of his arm. He wiped the sweat from his forehead. His face had hardened into his usual expression—flat, closed, impassive. "The hybrids need to be fed. The bonobos need fresh hay in their night house. And when you're finished with that, Vlad's house needs scrubbing out."

"Yes, sir," she said through gritted teeth.

A part of her loved the refuge and the animals within it—this place had been her home for as long as she could remember. But a bigger, angrier part of her resented it.

The needs of the refuge had taken over her life. After her mother left, her father enrolled her in online high school classes. He said she was safest at home, because even three years ago, the world was a dangerous place, with the crop blights and food shortages, the riots and domestic terrorist attacks, everything falling apart slowly and then all at once.

She had always helped out around her classwork. After graduating the previous spring, she had nothing keeping her from working all day. She couldn't afford the incredible expense of college. So she would help the keepers rake droppings and shovel in fresh straw, trying not to choke on the fetid stench; feed and water the animals; and make sure the wolves and bears weren't digging escape tunnels in their pens. During operating hours, she kept idiots from leaning on the wolves' fence or throwing French fries at the bears.

The fancy zoos had sanitation bots that did the grunt work. But a small, family-run refuge couldn't front that kind of cash. For the last month, it had been Raven, her father, and Zachariah. Now, she and her father were forced to do it all, just the two of them.

She watched her father stride away up the path, already dismissing her from his mind as he turned to his myriad other tasks. He'd always cared about this place and the animals more than people.

More than her mom, more than Zachariah, more than her.

She'd known he wouldn't remember. She might have forgiven him in the chaos of everything going on, except he'd never remembered. Not once. She told herself it didn't even hurt any more.

She turned back to the tiger house, her limbs heavy as lead. No matter what horrible things were happening in the outside world, her dad kept order in his domain. While Zachariah was dying, an afternoon mopping up tiger scat the size of her head lay ahead of her.

It didn't feel right. None of this felt right. She glanced up at the large tree in Vlad's enclosure. There were no heads hanging from the branches today. There'd been no heads since Zachariah had fallen ill.

She remembered being eight, and watching in horrified fascination as Zachariah hung bull heads he'd procured from the renderer on several branches eight to twelve feet high for the tiger's enrichment. Raven had never squealed or allowed herself to appear squeamish as Zachariah nonchalantly hooked a bloody ear, wedged horns in the fork between two branches, or hung the disembodied head upside down, a ghastly purple tongue poking from the thing's maw.

He had rubbed his hands together afterward and pointed at Vlad, who was springing high in the air and batting at the heads, intent on bringing them down for his next meal. "He's just working for his dinner like the rest of us, right?" Zachariah grinned at her. "It's nothing to be scared of. Simply a trick of the trade, little bird."

Zachariah had faced everything with a jovial fearlessness—he'd made Raven want to be the same way. Because of him, she hadn't had a single nightmare. As for her father, the thought that his eight-year-old daughter might be frightened of bloodied, severed heads hadn't even entered his mind.

She sucked in her breath, fighting the wave of sorrow flooding her veins. For a moment, she couldn't move from the surge of pain. And the other thought, dark and lethal, niggling at the corners of her mind.

Zachariah had coughed in her face. His infected, bloodied spittle had landed on her skin. Had microscopic droplets infiltrated her eye sockets? Her ears? If a single pathogenic particle slipped through the fibers of the mask and invaded her body, she was done for. In ten days' time, she'd be the one choking on her own blood, her organs melting into a toxic, insidious stew.

She shoved the thought down deep. There was nothing she could do about that now. What was done was done. She was sorry for Zachariah—deeply sorry. She grieved for him. But her plan hadn't changed. If anything, she was even more determined to get out.

Tonight, she was gone.

She straightened, steeling herself.

She pressed her hand to the bioscanner beside the locked, steel-reinforced door and pushed the button to lower the drop gate on the other side of the tiger house, which opened to Vlad's enclosure. The scanner beeped, and the service door swung open with a hiss. Before she went inside, she peeked around the corner at her pack, still ready and waiting.

The tiger house dens were six feet by twelve feet, with steel sheeting lining the walls, a welded mesh floor, and a steel-barred sliding drop gate. There were two chambers, though they had only one tiger.

The concrete floor of Vlad's den was covered with gristle, shredded fur, and the curved bones of horse ribs. This would take a while. She picked up the mop in the corner and took a shallow breath through her mouth. No matter how often it was scrubbed clean, the tiger house always stank with the fetid stench of raw meat, of death.

Another shout filtered down the hill, this time high and spiked with alarm.

Zachariah.

3

Raven dropped the mop and dashed outside. She shielded her eyes against the sun. At the top of the hill beside the timber wolf enclosure, the figure of her father bent over something lying in the pathway.

She sprinted up the hill, knowing what she would find but dreading it all the same. Her father glanced up as she halted beside him. His face looked like he'd aged ten years in the last ten days.

Zachariah lay sprawled at his feet, his limbs bent awkwardly beneath him, his features contorted in agony. Tears of blood stained his gaunt cheeks. His eyes were open, staring in frozen horror.

"Stay back," her father said.

She didn't point out that she'd already had contaminated bodily fluids sprayed at her face from less than a foot away. If the mask hadn't protected her, there was no point in taking precautions now. That horse had already left the barn.

Her father coughed and cleared his throat.

She knelt on the paved pathway beside the body. She wished he still looked like the Zachariah she'd known and loved, the one who was always grinning, his dark skin splitting into a hundred groves and wrinkles, who loved to ruffle her hair, who'd nicknamed her 'Little Bird' with great affection. "Is he—is he dead?"

Her father holstered the tranq gun. "If he isn't yet, he will be soon."

Her gaze snagged on the small gray tube with the orange top sticking out of Zachariah's concave chest. She reared back, her stomach wrenching. "What did you do?"

"He's no longer suffering," her father said, his voice flat, expressionless.

She jerked out the dart and stared at the syringe, the needle. She stumbled to her feet, reeling. "You gave him a dose intended for a tiger. You stopped his heart. You...you killed him."

"He was dying anyway."

It was true. She knew it was true. Still, the thought of pointing a gun, even a tranq gun, at a friend and then pulling the trigger set bile roiling in her stomach. She took a steadying breath, then another. "I didn't say goodbye."

"He wasn't himself anymore," her father said brusquely. "He could barely speak."

Still, revulsion filled her. It seemed so horrible, too horrible. She felt sick, her whole body going hot, then cold, then hot again. She thought of the virus, possibly inside her. The same virus that had done this to Zachariah.

"I should have kicked him out the moment he coughed."

She looked sharply at her father. "And abandon him when he most needed us? Where would he go? Who would feed him or bring him water? Who would take care of him?"

His face was strained, eyes glittering with anger. "He promised me he'd stay in the loft. He swore to me."

"He was sick! Crazed with pain."

"It was a mistake to allow him to stay."

"He is—was—family."

"No, he wasn't. He wasn't family, and he shouldn't have been here. I should've kicked him out like I wanted to." His gaze slanted at Raven, harsh and angry.

She was the one who'd begged to allow Zachariah to stay, who'd suggested the quarantine in the loft. It was her fault. Her father blamed her for this.

She shook her head, incredulous. Did her father even have a heart? Did he really even care about anyone else? He hadn't wept a single tear when her mother left. And he would've abandoned Zachariah—whom he'd known for fifteen years—without a backward glance or second thought.

Anger boiled up, but she shoved it down. It was useless. Her father didn't care about her outrage. "What now?" she asked. "We have to bury him. We have to...do something."

"I'll take care of it."

"We have to bury him," she repeated.

Her father glanced down at the body, eyes narrowing. "I said I'll take care of it."

"That's not the same thing." Her father was unsentimental to the extreme. Who knew what his idea of 'taking care of it' meant. "He needs to be buried. We have to show our respects."

"Fine." Her father expelled a sharp breath. "I will bury him."

"I'll help you."

"No, you won't." His voice was steel.

"He was my friend, too—"

"I said no!" He coughed again, a deep, horrible hacking that shook his shoulders. He pulled down his mask to wipe his mouth with the back of his arm.

Raven stared at the mask, aghast. It wasn't white like it was

25

supposed to be. Instead, it held a pinkish hue. Her gaze dropped to his right arm. His faded, long-sleeved plaid shirt was speckled with red droplets.

Understanding struck her, sharp and swift as an axe blade. She saw suddenly what she hadn't noticed with the world in chaos, Zachariah's illness, the never-ending tasks of caring for the animals, dread over her impending birthday, and her own plans for escape—which suddenly seemed ridiculous, empty, and selfish.

The sweat leaking down her father's face, beading on his forehead, his lower lip, staining the underarms of his khaki shirt. Sweat on a cool day. The bruised circles beneath his eyes, which she'd assumed were from lack of sleep. The coughing—she'd believed it was simply his asthma.

And the smell. Which she'd barely noticed until now, but Vlad had. Vlad, who was still frantically pacing behind the fence at the bottom of the hill, his lips pulled back from his two-inch fangs as he snarled and shook his head, unable to rid himself of the stench of something sharp and pungent, a sour, noxious scent that turned her stomach and filled her with dread.

The stink of sickness.

Her father was infected.

4

Raven slumped in a metal chair several feet from her father's bed. Afternoon light slanted through the windows, bathing the room in warm shadows. Her father groaned, tossing uncomfortably, his limbs slick with sweat, his face gaunt, eyes hollowed.

"Ten feet," he'd growled when she tried to come closer. The CDC broadcasts had recommended remaining ten feet from any suspected infected persons. After a while, they simply advised survivors to stay away from everyone.

She brought him a damp washcloth to press against his fevered forehead anyway, and a pitcher of water for his aching throat and rasping cough. Without power, the water and the washcloth were both warm. She couldn't even give him ice for his parched thirst.

It wasn't enough. How could it possibly be enough?

She stared dully at the bare, log-cabin walls. It had been a day since she'd realized the truth. Her father, who had hidden his symptoms and barreled through the pain, determined to endure, had collapsed at the breakfast table that morning.

She knew what the vloggers had said in the newsfeeds, the parade of scientists and virologists and CDC experts, their technical terms masking the true horror: the Hydra virus was designed to destroy the human body from the inside out.

After initial infection, there was a seventy-two-hour incubation period. On days two to four, mild coughing and sneezing set in, just enough to efficiently spread the contagion.

Then, as the disease advanced through the later stages, came the high fevers, breathing difficulties, chronic coughing, and hemorrhaging from the mouth, eyes, and ears on days ten through twelve. Between days ten and fourteen came respiratory failure and death. Some infected experienced what Zachariah had—an adrenaline surge during the last stage, the virus's last-ditch effort to spread itself.

A small percentage of the population was immune. For the rest, the mortality rate was one hundred percent. There was no cure, no escape once you were infected. No reprieve. No hope.

Which meant she was watching her father die.

Raven hunched over a small pine log she'd chosen from the stack of firewood next to the fireplace. She scraped at the wood with numb, trembling fingers, barely seeing the object taking shape in her hands. Several times, her fingers slipped. The blade nicked her thumb, bit into her knuckle.

She wiped the blood on her pants and kept working, breathing hard, cutting and cutting, carving deep into the soft wood, wood shavings tinged with red falling into her lap, drifting to the floor like shriveled petals. The feelings boiling inside her were too big, too horrible to look at head on.

Her legs were shaking, aching to run, to flee, to escape this awful stench of sickness and her father's awful rattling breaths. The darkness closed in on her, seeping into her skin, her pores, her cells.

The sight of him lying there, quivering and helpless, body wracked in pain, sent a hot spike through her gut. She'd never seen him anything but capable, self-contained, strong and stoic, needing nothing and no one. Now he was weak, suffering, a stranger with her father's face.

He may not have been the father she'd wanted—but he was the father she had. He was dying. And she was helpless.

She closed her hands over the wooden bird she'd carved—a raven. One rough-hewn wing was stained a pale red from the nick in her finger. When she had been small, only four or five, she used to collect things—stray buttons, ribbons, pretty stones, bottle caps, magnets—anything shiny and bright and lovely. Her father had called her a little *karasu*, a raven. Her mother had laughed merrily— back when she still laughed—and the name had stuck.

Her real name was Emiko, but no one had called her that in years. She'd loved that her father had given her a nickname. As a girl, she'd adored it, clung to it like one of the bright little pebbles she tucked under her pillow, hoping with all her heart that it meant he loved her.

A small groan escaped Raven's lips. She blinked away the burning in her eyes, shoved the knife and the carving into her cargo pocket, and stood abruptly, nearly knocking over her chair. "I'm going into town. I'll find a doctor."

Her father opened his eyes, his face clenching from the effort of speaking. "There are...none."

She knew he was right. She knew billions were dead, and those who weren't were taking care of themselves, their own families. She knew the hospitals had refused to admit any more sick people weeks ago. And even if there were doctors and hospitals, they wouldn't be able to save her father. They hadn't been able to save anyone.

And yet her fear was an irrational thing. She clung to the old world with desperation. After all, she hadn't left Haven herself. She hadn't seen it with her own eyes. Surely it wasn't that bad. Surely there were still doctors and surgeons and medical centers and people going to work and coming home and kids riding hoverboards and playing virtual reality games all day and stores with shelves full of food and medicine.

"Then medicine! Something to ease the pain!" she choked out.

"It's not safe." He turned his head slowly to look at her. His dark eyes were glassy. His sweat-damp hair was slick against his forehead. "I'll be fine."

She let out a bitter laugh at the black irony. "I'll be back before dark. I'll make sure the animals are taken care of."

"Don't take stupid risks," he growled. "Not for anyone."

She'd heard that argument a hundred times. *Keep to yourself. Keep your head down. Take care of yourself, first and only.* That may be the way her father lived, but it didn't mean she had to live the same way. Not now. Not like this. She'd obeyed him, only to watch her mother leave and Zachariah die.

She'd been hours from leaving her father for good—for months, maybe years. But that was leaving by choice. That was leaving someone healthy and alive, someone you knew would continue to move and breathe and do all the things they'd always done while you were gone.

This was different. This was a giant hand reaching inside the cage of her ribs and wrenching her heart out, squeezing the life from her veins while she watched.

"It won't take long, I promise. I'll come right back." She hadn't left Haven in weeks, since before the Hydra virus reared its ugly head. First, she hadn't had a reason to. And then her father hadn't allowed it.

"I forbid it," he croaked.

"I'm sorry," she said.

His fingers scraped the bed sheets like claws, tendons bulging in his neck as a wave of agony pulsed through his body. She watched, frozen and helpless, sickened and horrified but unable to look away. Looking away felt like a betrayal, of both herself and her father.

The pain released him, and he sagged against the mattress, panting. She grabbed the damp washcloth from the nightstand and tried to press it to his forehead, but he waved her away.

He pointed a frail, trembling finger at his dresser beneath the window. The tranquilizer gun lay atop the dresser, steeped in golden sunlight. "You want to ease my suffering? That'll do it."

"No," she said, recoiling. "No."

"I want you to do it." He took several ragged, rasping breaths. "I'm asking you to do it."

"I—I can't."

He worked his jaw, like he sometimes did when he was chewing on words he'd rather keep to himself. "Let me go on my own terms."

Revulsion settled in her stomach like a block of ice. She shook her head, tasting acid in the back of her throat. "I'll be back. With medicine."

"Raven!" he croaked. "Don't you go!"

But she was already headed for the door, frantic with the desire to escape that claustrophobic room full of the stench of sickness, swirling with the whispers of grief and bitterness and regret.

"Take the tranq," he said behind her.

She stiffened for a moment, but she obeyed. She pivoted, seized the thing from the dresser, and fled the room.

She rushed through the shadow-darkened living room, pausing only to grab her dad's SmartFlex on the shabby coffee table so she could use the car. She'd already put one of the solar lamps on the nightstand in her father's room next to the water pitcher. He'd have light even if she came back after dark. They saved the generator for the electrified fences to keep the carnivores inside where they belonged.

Too many horrible thoughts churned through her mind. Her father was dying. He wanted her to kill him. She hated the thought of his suffering; she hated the thought of aiming a gun and pulling the trigger even less. That it was a dart and not a bullet meant little. The end result was the same. Quick and sudden death.

She pushed those thoughts out of her mind. She needed to focus on one single thing at a time. Step A led to step B led to step C.

If she found strong enough painkillers, he wouldn't need the tranquilizer. She would get medication to ease her father's pain. Then she would tackle what needed to be done next.

Raven hurried out the door.

5

The town of Clay Creek was small and dingy by anyone's standards. Population: 1,800. One crappy McDonalds. A grocery store. A mechanic shop. Two dreary gas stations that had seen better days. The nearest mall, not that Raven cared, was over thirty miles away. Ditto for the nearest big box store.

Even on its best days, no one could say the town was busy. Today, it was a ghost town. Only a few people hurried along the sidewalks, heads down, masks covering their faces, gloved hands shoved deep into the pockets of their jackets to ward off the late afternoon chill.

Most of the sagging storefronts were closed, many with two-by-fours barring their front doors. The windows of Dewie's Barber and Shave were smashed in, the ancient red-and-white-striped barber pole knocked to the weed-infested sidewalk.

Raven had passed several dozen abandoned cars on the twenty-mile drive in. There were more abandoned cars, several on the side of the road, one with both its doors hanging open; another parked at a stop sign, with no one inside.

She drove to the doctor's office first, a two-story brick building where she'd had every shot and check-up she could remember. It too had been broken into. Every window was shattered. The door had been taken right off its hinges.

By the time she pulled her father's battered fifteen-year-old forest-green Toyota into the empty parking lot of Maxwell Family Pharmaceuticals, the hairs on the back of her neck were standing on end. There were no broken windows. No graffiti on the brick exterior walls. The sidewalk was swept. A hand-scrawled sign taped to the front door said: "Still Open, 12-4 Daily."

Clay Creek was a small town, a safe town. Nothing like the chaotic, rioting cities. Still, the best thing was to get in and out as quickly as possible.

She glanced at the tranq gun on the passenger side seat. She knew how to handle a gun. She'd gone hunting dozens of times. But the idea of using one against other people turned her stomach.

She pushed her mask up over her nose and tugged on a fresh pair of disposable gloves her dad kept in the glove compartment. She stored the tranq gun inside, next to the box of gloves. It was there if she needed it.

She shut and locked the car and hurried past several motorcycles parked outside the pharmacy. The bell tinkled as she opened the door and slipped inside. The shadows were deep, but there was enough daylight streaming through the windows to see by. The small shop smelled like pine air freshener and aftershave. She went straight to the back counter.

Phil Maxwell, the owner, and his son Carl, who was in his mid-thirties, stood behind the counter. They both wore masks and gloves.

"I don't have much left," Phil said, barely glancing at her as his gaze fixed on the four bikers, who stuck out like bulls in a china shop. The bikers—burly, tattooed—were hunched together against the far wall, prying at the junk food machine and swearing when the printer jammed.

Raven scanned the nearly empty shelves. She licked her dry lips beneath her mask. "My dad is sick. He needs something that can help him."

A flash of pity shone in Phil's eyes. "Kioko Nakamura was a good man. I'm sorry to hear that."

"He's not dead yet," she said, her heart constricting. It was a stupid thing to say, but she couldn't help it.

"He won't get better," Carl said. He was a short, toady man with a snubbed, flattened face and dull eyes. He always stared suspiciously at everyone under twenty, like he longed to accuse them of shoplifting or some other nefarious activity. Raven had never cared for him.

She forced her voice to remain calm. "I know that. But he's in pain. He's suffering. I don't have a prescription, but..."

Phil sighed and ran his hands through the halo of white hair that ringed his balding head. "I've been keeping this place open for just that reason. Carl, go back and grab some oxycodone."

Carl scowled. "That's our last bottle. Our livelihood. All that's left—"

Phil's expression tensed. Shadows pooled beneath his eyes. "Just do it." As Carl obeyed with a huff, Phil dragged his gaze back to Raven. "When's the last time you had power?"

"A few weeks."

He sighed heavily. "Us either. Your generators holding okay?"

Raven nodded. She caught sight of the fridge in the back containing all the medications that needed to remain cold. The doors were wrapped in chains and a large padlock. "And yours?"

"It's lasting, so far. Things'll get worse before they get better, mark my words."

"You hear about all the rioting in Atlanta and Chicago?" Carl plunked the bottle down on the counter between them. His eyes glittered with something Raven couldn't quite read. Was it smug satisfaction? Morbid excitement? "They don't even have workers to clean up all the dead bodies in the cities. The police and National Guard are fallin' apart at the seams, literally. Either all dead or leavin' to protect their families. That's what I would do. Let the government try to clean up their own damn mess for once."

Raven just stared at him, at a loss for words. Carl was only one of the many reasons she preferred an isolated cabin in the woods to the cruel, indifferent world of people.

Phil handed her the bottle. "Find yourself a safe place and stay there, you hear me?"

"Thanks." She took the bottle and shoved it in her pants' pocket. "How much for this?"

"For you? No charge. Just remember this and pay it forward any way you can. I have a feeling folks are going to need all the help they can get."

Gratitude filled her. She blinked and managed a smile. "Thank you."

She turned for the door just as two more bikers pulled up outside. They wore semi-automatic rifles strapped to their chests. They were both tall and olive-skinned, maybe in their late twenties.

The first one had black hair yanked back in a ponytail. He was gaunt, his body long and sharp as a knife. The other moved with liquid grace, like a dancer—or a panther. Their faces were lean and hard, their eyes glinting dangerously.

Unease shivered up her spine. Her gut tightened. She'd grown up around predators. She recognized one when she saw it.

Instinct made her sidestep and shrink behind a five-foot shelf housing conditioners, shampoos, razors, and shaving cream. She peered around the corner as the two bikers swaggered in, the bell tinkling in warning. The three men already inside sauntered to the counter.

"How can I help you, gentlemen?" Phil asked.

"We need all the painkillers and antibiotics you got, Pops," said the skinny, pony-tailed one. He wore a leather vest with a skull emblazoned on the back.

"*Please,*" said the second guy, the one that reminded her of a panther. His coal-black hair framed a long, angular face as he gave a languid, mocking smile. He scratched his goateed chin and perused the empty shelves with a disinterested, heavy-lidded gaze.

"We're happy to give you a few," Phil said, still polite, his voice tight. The five thugs with guns looming over him were intimidating. He was trying unsuccessfully not to let them see his fear. "We're rationing the supply as long as we can so more people get what they need. With the hospitals closed, this is the only medical care people can get."

"You mistake our politeness," said a third man, this one blond with hair shorn close to his skull. A scorpion tattoo snaked up his neck. His squinty eyes were hooded in his fleshy, shovel-shaped face. Several empty backpacks were slung across his shoulder.

He placed the backpacks on the counter. Then he lifted his rifle and set it down beside the backpacks, so it faced Phil and Carl. He stroked the barrel fondly, his lips peeling back from his teeth in a sinister smile. "As you can see, we aren't asking."

6

Raven crouched lower, shrinking to appear as small as possible. Her pulse throbbed against her neck. Her brain screamed at her to flee, but there was nowhere to go, no way to sneak out without drawing attention to herself.

"Now, let's try this again," the biker with the scorpion tattoo said. "Fill these backpacks with everything you've got." He paused, a sly grin playing across his lips. "*Please* and *thank you*."

"You can't just take our things." Carl scowled, his voice rising. "That's against the law."

Panther guy half-turned, his hand shielding his eyes as if he were looking for something. "I don't see any law here, do you, Scorpio?"

"There are no laws now," said Scorpio, the biker with the scorpion tattoo. "No police, no judges, no courts. Nothing. It's all gone to hell."

"This is a civilized society!" Carl whined.

"Oh, I assure you we are quite civilized," Ponytail said. Slowly, with exaggerated movements, he turned and hocked a massive loogie onto the floor. Panther guy laughed darkly.

Raven tensed. They were baiting him, entertaining themselves, but Carl was too stupid to see it.

Carl's face purpled, his jaw pulsing. "You can't just go around stealing because you feel like it, taking a man's livelihood right out from under him. It's thugs like you who ruined this country in the first place!"

Several of the bikers stiffened. Panther guy's smile dissolved. "Shut your trap and give us what we want."

"I suggest you listen to Ryker," Ponytail drawled.

Phil shot his son a warning look. "Carl."

Carl ignored it. He pointed his finger in Panther guy's—Ryker's —face. "You won't get away with this, you filthy son of a—"

In one swift, fluid movement, Ryker pulled a pistol from his holster and aimed it at Carl. There was no surprise in the other bikers' faces. No hatred or even anger. Even Ryker's expression was smooth, his black eyes dull and flinty. "I'm hungry, tired, and I've had a long day. Test me one more time—"

Phil stuck both hands in the air. "We mean no harm. We'll get you what you've asked for."

"No, we won't." Carl was shaking, his eyes bulging, but he would not shut his stupid mouth. "We're not letting you thieving scumbags steal what's rightfully ours."

He didn't understand that they were the predators, and he the prey. He didn't understand that they wouldn't have bothered with him if he'd stayed still and small, if he hadn't turned aggressive himself, challenging their dominance—the one thing men like these would not let slide.

Scorpio sneered. "You little pissant."

"You think you scare me?" Carl snarled. "You come in here with your big guns and—"

Ryker shot Carl point-blank in the face.

The blast of the gunshot exploded against Raven's ears. She clasped both hands over her mouth to contain the whimper of shock.

Carl's body dropped to the floor behind the counter. Blood splattered everywhere—the counter, the printed candy rack. Phil's pristine white lab coat, his face, his mask, the white puff of hair ringing his scalp.

Phil stood frozen beside his son's body, his arms still raised, his eyes wide and startled.

Scorpio grunted as he wiped a faint spray of blood off his face with the flap of his shirt. "Did you have to do that?"

"I did," Ryker said, his face impassive, his gaze flat. "He offended my...honor."

Scorpio shook his head. "Cerberus won't be pleased."

Ryker swiveled and pointed the gun at Phil. He sneered, his features contorting into an expression of derision, but there was something missing, something empty. His eyes were dull as lead. "We better not leave any witnesses, then."

Raven shrank back against the shelves, bumping the lowest one with her knee. A shampoo bottle wavered. She seized it before it clattered to the tile floor.

She held her breath, her heart thumping, but no one turned around. No one but Phil knew she was there.

"I've got this," said a younger guy she hadn't noticed before. He'd hung back silently until now. Metal glinted at his lip and brow. He looked maybe twenty, tallish and lanky, with a head of short russet-red hair, a narrow, pointy face and cunning eyes, reminding her distinctly of a fox. A very handsome fox.

He lifted the rifle slung over his shoulder and aimed it at Phil.

"Get what we asked for, or I'll blow your kneecaps, then your ankles, then your hands, one by one, and then we'll watch you bleed out and die like a stuck pig."

"You heard Damien." Ryker's lip curled in faint amusement. He holstered his own gun. "Do what he says, and maybe you'll live to bury your son."

Raven waited, every muscle taut, fear and adrenaline pumping through her, as Phil turned without a word. Trembling, he bagged up the remaining medications.

"Faster!" Damien snarled, gesturing with the gun.

Ryker slapped Damien on the back, grinning. "Lookie there. The young pup is coming into his own!"

Damien gave a hard little grin, his eyes unreadable. "Get the damn meds, old man."

Minutes that felt like hours later, the bikers had what they wanted. Phil crammed the bottles and boxes into the backpack with trembling fingers. "That—that's it."

Damien cursed at him. The other men laughed, jeering and mocking.

Phil cowered. "Please," he whispered over and over. "Please, please, please."

"You're just a pathetic old man," Damien snarled. He jabbed the barrel of the rifle once into Phil's chest. Raven cringed, half-expecting him to shoot Phil just for the fun of it. Phil went rigid, closing his eyes, as if he expected the same thing. Maybe a part of him wanted it, so he wouldn't have to bear the pain of living in a shattered world without his son.

But Damien turned away with a dismissive sneer. "He's not worth the bullet. This place stinks. Let's go."

The bikers strode loudly from the pharmacy, knocking the few remaining items off the shelves, bulging backpacks slung over their

42

shoulders. Raven shrank back, heart roaring in her ears, but none of them bothered to look down.

After a minute, their motorcycles roared to life, and they peeled out of the parking lot.

Raven forced herself to stand, her legs wobbly, adrenaline still icing her veins. She rushed to the counter. On the other side, Phil squatted on the tile floor next to his son, weeping. It was a private moment, one she had no part of. She backed away to give him privacy. There was nothing she—or anyone—could do for Carl.

She swiped her dad's SmartFlex cuff on her wrist and activated it with her thumbprint bio-signature—her dad had added her to his account so she could access the car. She forced her voice to remain calm, though she felt anything but. "Call 911."

"Service cannot be reached," the SmartFlex chimed.

"Try again." She got the same answer. She tried the local police and the county sheriff. Still nothing. She swallowed hard. What had she expected?

It felt like the floor was cracking open beneath her, and she was falling, falling, falling, with no bottom in sight. It was true, then. There really was no more law, no more police. Here, at least. Maybe everywhere.

Phil stood. He wiped at his face with the back of his hand. He stared at his streaked fingers, stained with his son's blood. "You should go home. Stay there. This is no place for a girl."

She wanted to say this was no place for anyone, but her words turned to ash in her mouth. She wanted to comfort him, but there was nothing to say, nothing that would mean a thing against this meaningless act of violence. Instead, she nodded mutely, turned, and ran from the shadows of the store into the cool, late afternoon sunlight.

She'd barely reached the car when the back of her neck prickled.

Someone was watching her. She glanced down the street. At least ten motorcycles were parked at the bank. The bikers were inside—they'd smashed the glass doors—except for one.

Ryker leaned against his bike, smoking a cigarette. He lounged languid as a cat poised to strike, his gaze fixed on her. Their eyes met for a brief, electric moment. Those eyes were dull, lifeless, like hollow black pits.

She jerked the car door open, stumbled into her seat, punched the auto-drive button, and sat back with a shudder as the car pulled out of the pharmacy parking lot. The entire ride home, she couldn't stop shivering.

The bikers were right.

The world had gone to hell.

7

By the time Raven returned to the lodge an hour later, the Toyota's electric battery was completely drained. She plugged it into the charger, but the power was still out.

The electrified fences in the park had automatic back-up generators that would last a few more weeks. She didn't want to turn on the one for the lodge, not unless she absolutely had to. If the power wasn't coming back on for months, maybe longer, the generators were all she had.

She brought the tranq gun into the house but set it on the coffee table. She didn't want it in his room, anywhere near him. The pills would help. The pills would take away his pain.

She entered the doorway to her father's bedroom, gripping the bottle of painkillers so tightly her knuckles went white. "Dad?"

He didn't answer.

The room was filled with heavy shadows, dusk staining the windows. She slipped the mask over her mouth and nose and went to his bedside, flipping on the solar lamp.

His chest rose and fell in jerky, uneven movements, his breathing raspy. He moaned and writhed, tangling the rumpled bedding, the sheets damp. The room stank of sweat and sickness.

But that wasn't the worst thing. A drop of blood rimmed his outer ear. Another dot of crimson stained the hollow beneath his right eye.

Hemorrhaging from multiple orifices...the last stage before the end. Before death.

How could she not have seen it? How could he have been so sick and stayed on his feet? The fever stage burned over 105 degrees. She remembered that from the CDC health alerts. Why had he purposefully kept this from her?

"Dad," she said. She cleared her throat. "Dad. I got it. I got you medicine."

He groaned and opened his eyes. They were glassy and threaded with scarlet. "Raven," he croaked.

She fumbled with the bottle and spilled three pills into her palm. She added two more, to make sure. "This will help you feel better."

His face darkened. "I told you not to go. I told you what to do."

She swallowed. "I'm not—I can't do that. But I got these. They'll ease the pain, I promise."

She managed to slip the pills in his mouth, lifting his head, pressing a glass of water to his lips and getting him to swallow them down. His head fell back against the sweaty pillow.

He stared up at her like she was a stranger, his eyes so bloodshot they looked crimson. The fever-heat emanated off him in waves. "You start coughing, you know what to do."

She shook her head. "Stop. Don't talk about that."

"There's enough etorphine to stop your heart."

She pressed her lips together. "I got it."

He heaved a ragged breath. "Do the animals first. Before you do it yourself. You know where the guns are."

Her mind revolted from the thought. "You should rest."

"Don't be weak."

"I said I got it."

He turned to the wall as he hacked up a bloody, phlegmy cough. She handed him a clean washcloth. He wiped his mouth. For several minutes, he didn't speak. The sound of his ragged breathing filled the room.

"Dad—"

"I was weak," he barked, his face contorting. "I was weak and let Zachariah stay. He came after you. Now you've got it, too."

"It wasn't his fault," she said, her chest constricting. She'd never seen him like this before, never heard him talk about anything beyond lessons and instructions and orders. "And you don't know that."

"Don't be stupid. I saw what I saw. So did you. I should've kicked him out long ago...never should've let him stay."

"He was your friend."

"He wasn't anyone," her father snarled. "That's the mistake... never trust anyone...'specially the ones who call themselves *friend*."

This wasn't how she wanted things to go. He was dying. She should say something important. Something that meant something. But her words failed her.

Her father groaned. She forced herself to look at him, at the mask of pain contorting his face into someone unrecognizable. But then, she'd never really known her father. No one had.

Her gaze strayed to the medal of valor sitting in a velvet box atop his dresser, gathering dust. Her mother always said he'd never been the same after he came back from the war. Back when Raven was only three, after the Hand of God terrorist group set off several suitcase nukes, he'd served as a peacekeeper in the Democratic Republic of Congo.

He was flying a chopper full of medical aid to wounded soldiers when it crashed over the Congo Basin. He survived in the jungle for ninety-seven days. He said once that he wished he'd made it to one hundred.

Her mother had insisted on displaying the medal. Her father had hated it. Once, when Raven was around ten, she'd made the mistake of admiring it. She'd called her father a hero.

He'd turned away, his hard face twisting in revulsion. "It is not a heroic thing to survive."

She'd never figured out whether it was the award itself he found so repellent, or what he'd had to do to receive it. She knew only the barest of facts.

Four men had survived the crash deep in the Congo jungle. Only one had made it out.

Her father had returned thirty pounds lighter, gaunt and starving, an infected knife wound festering across his right bicep and no explanation for how he had suffered it. Her mother claimed he was never the same, after. Raven was too young to remember him before. Being alone like that, surviving any way you had to, it changed a person. It changed him.

"Your father thinks a man is an island," her mom had said once, right before she left. "He *wants* to be an island. He's cut everyone out for his entire life. He thinks it makes him stronger, but he's wrong, Raven. He's the loneliest man I ever met."

Now there was only her dad and Raven. Soon, it would only be Raven.

Her insides twisted. Her mouth tasted of copper. Zachariah was dead. Her father was dying. And she was alone. Totally, completely alone.

"What am I supposed to do?" she whispered. "How am I supposed to do this?"

But her father's face had gone slack. Finally, mercifully, he'd drifted into a drug-induced sleep.

She backed away, her legs like lead, and sank into a faded orange armchair she'd once loved for its deep, downy cushions. Now it was just old, dirty, and smelled like moths.

Her backpack sat in her room. The cabin was waiting for her. The animals still needed to be fed. The bonobos' night house had never been cleaned. And she was exhausted, so incredibly weary.

To keep herself awake, she forced herself to look around the bedroom. Like him, it was spartan—a lumpy mattress, an old computer-integrated desk, a nightstand, the orange armchair, the log walls bare of pictures or sentimentality. An ancient television sat on the dresser. No holoscreens or wall screen for her dad.

He never watched television anyway. He was always in the woods, hiking or hunting or with the animals, which was usually what this room smelled like—pine and dirt and dank fur.

It had been different when her mom was here. But those memories were fading like old-fashioned print photos; she could no longer remember the particular scent of her mother's perfume.

Some days, even the image of her mother blurred in her mind, and she couldn't recall the shape her mom's smile took when she was genuinely happy, or whether it was her left or right eyebrow that scrunched like a caterpillar when she was upset—which was often.

She did remember the depressions, remembered creeping into one of the guest rooms to discover the lump of her mother's body beneath the covers, the room shadowed and dark, the air thick with misery.

Raven swallowed hard. She ran her fingers over the soft ridges of her mask. It was harder to breathe with it on in here, in the claustrophobic air that felt like it was losing oxygen by the minute.

She shifted uncomfortably, her father's oversized SmartFlex digging into her wrist. She unsnapped the two-inch wide faux leather cuff and unfolded it, turning it over and over in her hands. She hadn't checked the vlogs in almost two weeks. She'd been too busy keeping Haven going.

She thought of Clay Creek, the eerily empty streets and shops; of Carl's face imploding before her eyes. The arterial spray of blood, so impossibly bright; the black hole opening up beneath her feet when she realized the police weren't coming, that maybe there weren't any police anymore. Of the flinty gleam in those bikers' eyes, their casual cruelty, their absolute belief that they would get away with it, that there was no longer anyone to stop them.

Her stomach cramped. She activated her dad's SmartFlex. She'd let the battery die on hers. It was mostly useless now anyway.

Her dad's data appeared as a digital overlay. It hovered above her hands, three-dimensional, tinged bluish and slightly transparent —nothing but statistics about the animals, bills that needed paying, health updates that were overdue.

She swiped the newsfeed bar. No new posts. The latest vlogs were almost three weeks old, which was almost more terrifying. When she tried to search the internet, nothing came up. "Error. Please try again," the Smartflex chimed. She gave up on the search and scrolled through all the old alerts instead.

Schools districts closing, by county and, later, by state. Big businesses and corporations shutting their doors. The Centers for Disease Control and the World Health Organization releasing health alert after health alert, warning after warning. Videos of riots outside hospitals and medical centers. Whole communities burning. Thousands shut inside quarantine areas lined with fences topped with barbed wire. The sick lining up outside FEMA tent cities. And the bodies. Bodies everywhere. By the thousands, the hundreds of thousands. Mass graves. And worse.

The President gave repeated addresses in attempts to calm the people. She declared martial law along with an emergency bill requiring every citizen be chipped to detect even microscopic virus levels.

Her father had insisted neither of them get the implant. "Let them come to us, then," he'd growled. "Seems to me the government's got bigger problems." And he was right. It was the one thing he and her mother had always agreed on: their mutual distrust of the government.

Raven scrolled through more vid feeds she'd already seen. Soldiers manning checkpoints and guarding quarantine zones, refusing to allow people in or out. More rioting, more burning. Looting and violence. The National Guard called in to quell outraged uprisings. International air and naval travel banned. Then national, then state and county. Then it didn't matter.

Mayors and governors, senators and presidents, prime ministers, princes and tyrants, they died as easily as the homeless, the poverty-stricken, the children. Police and soldiers either died in droves or abandoned their posts to protect their own families. Cities and urban centers fell to gangs, brutality, and violence.

She swiped on the last report: "The death toll has now reached four billion," a shell-shocked Hispanic woman said, her hands clenched over the broadcasting desk. "An epidemiologist at the CDC just released a projection model indicating that within the next thirty to sixty days, ninety-four to ninety-six percent of the population will be wiped out. Experts at the World Health Organization are working around the clock to find a vaccine and have made significant headway..."

The report was dated seventeen days ago.

Then, nothing.

No more reports. No more newsfeeds or vloggers. No more internet.

Fresh fear stabbed the base of her spine. A tremor went through her, like she was standing too close to the edge of a cliff. The numbers were impossible to comprehend. Not until she'd gone to Clay Creek, seen the town for herself. Not until she'd met the bikers.

It was the end of the world.

Right here, as she sat next to her dying father, the whole world was crumbling, dying right along with him.

Her mind kept wanting to reject it, deny it, keep on pretending as long as she could—until she couldn't anymore.

It was too much to take in, too much for one person to bear; she was finally, irrevocably alone. She was getting what she'd wanted. To be alone. To be a loner, solitary, surrounded by silence.

But not like this, her panicked mind whispered. *Never like this.*

She got up slowly, her muscles aching, and walked to her dad's bed. His legs thrashed, twisting in the bed sheets. Sweat drenched his ashen face. His whole body was rigid. Tendons stood out on his neck. His eyes were deep, bruised hollows.

Blood dripped like tears down his cheeks.

She pulled the armchair right up to the bed, ten-feet rule be damned, and hunched beside him, keeping vigil long into the night.

She kept waiting for his last words, for him to finally look at her and say something important, maybe some last-minute advice on surviving the apocalypse. Or what she really hoped for—an *I was wrong,* or *I wish things were different,* or most of all, an *I love you.*

But in the end, in death he was the same as he was in life—reticent, private, unknowable.

Twelve hours later, her father was dead.

8

T he next day, Raven buried her father where he'd buried Zachariah less than three days ago.

She had no coffin, no funeral home to call. This was the new world: a twisted, funhouse version of the old world, the two hundred intervening years erased in only a few desperate, horrifying weeks.

It was difficult, exhausting work, punching the shovel though the red Georgia clay again and again and again. By the end of it, she was trembling and sweating, her damp and sticky T-shirt clinging to her chest and back, her palms stinging with blisters.

She'd buried one of her wolf carvings with him, along with an old family picture she'd found stuffed in a drawer. It had been taken in front of the wolves' enclosure when she was six. Her little round face had been shining, joyous, but even then, her dad was looking at something off-camera, distracted. Her mom's expression was tight, pinched, her eyes distant, already dreaming of somewhere else.

Happiness had never been a defining trait of her family. She remembered three people bumping around within the same four walls, never touching. She remembered silence. Lots and lots of silence. Not the living, vibrant kind, filled with insects and wind and animal sounds, but the oppressive silence weighted with all the words hungry to be spoken. They never were.

Raven patted down the last shovelful of red dirt and clay, her arms aching. The trees rustled above her, their crimson, orange, and yellow leaves curling at the edges, ready to die. She was deep in the woods, about a mile outside the perimeter of the park.

Last night, the timber wolves had begun to howl. Somehow, they had known her dad was gone. It was different from their usual howling to communicate with each other. This was a chorus of grief. They sang in sorrowful, haunting concert, sending up a keening wail that echoed, eerie and beautiful.

"I'm sorry," she said to the dirt. Her eyes stung. Her chest was too tight. Some giant hand was squeezing, squeezing, squeezing the life out of her. She couldn't catch her breath. The ground kept tilting dangerously beneath her feet.

She didn't know what to say or how to say it. She didn't know any poignant poems or appropriate songs. Nothing meaningful would come. Only a dull sense of despair, a numbness spreading from the center of her being.

She resented her father. She also loved him. "I know that you tried."

She turned away from the graves—her father's and Zachariah's—and made her way through the forest back to Haven.

She had wanted to escape to find solitude, but now that solitude —and safety—was here. Solitude maybe, but not peace and quiet. The bonobos were screeching their displeasure, the bobcat yowling unhappily, the zebra braying and barking, the wolves growling with hunger.

Her father had bought Haven Wildlife Refuge when he'd

returned from the war when Raven was five. It housed one tiger, two black bears, six timber wolves, two hybrid wolves, four bonobos, two porcupines, one bobcat, three red foxes, four otters, one zebra, two ostriches, one eagle, four peacocks, two tortoises, two dozen flamingos, flocks of geese and ducks, and a fifteen-foot long boa constrictor named Winston.

Every one of those animals was hungry—with the possible exception of Winston. Most of them ate an enormous amount of food. None of the animals had been fed yesterday or today.

She desperately needed a distraction from the grief encircling her throat like chains. Here it was, the animals demanding her attention whether she wanted them or not.

"Okay," she muttered. "Hold your horses. I'm coming."

She circled around the four-foot wrought-iron perimeter fence to the front of the park, skirting the parking lot and coming through the front entrance. She closed and locked the gates.

There was no such thing as visitors anymore, but her father had drilled caution into her. Every night since the president's first catastrophic address, her father had patrolled Haven's perimeter with his hunting rifle. The sight of the gun had infuriated Vlad every single evening.

The flagstone walking paths took a serpentine route through the oblong-shaped park. In the center of the park sprawled the enormous walk-in enclosure, featuring the lake with the flamingos, various feathered fowl, the pens for the tortoises, and the peacocks, though they were always escaping into the general park.

Near the entrance were the ancient turnstiles, the Grizzly Grill restaurant, souvenir shop and bathrooms, and the six-suite log lodge that her dad had converted into their living quarters.

Whoever built the place thirty years ago hadn't put much thought into it. The food storage and prep sheds—including the meat house—were only twenty yards behind the lodge. When the wind blew the wrong way, she kept her bedroom window closed.

Raven went into the concrete block building that contained the frozen meat for the carnivores—the tiger, wolves, bobcat, and bears. The walk-in freezer held the two hundred pounds of meat Zachariah picked up every few weeks from a local renderer—mostly calves, sheep, and pigs; occasionally bulls or horses.

Zachariah hadn't gone since he had gotten sick. The freezer was nearly empty.

Her gaze swept the rest of the room: a steel table for chopping meat, a huge steel sink, a wooden block stuck with gigantic butcher knives. A chest freezer full of rats for the birds-of-prey and Winston. Her father always called them ratsicles.

A memory struck her—her father as she'd so often seen him, straddling a calf carcass, brandishing a gigantic, bloodied knife, entrails and blood puddling around his boots as he grinned broadly, right at home in the gross muck.

She blinked the sudden sting from her eyes and checked the generator; still working. It would last another week, maybe two. She added finding more propane to her internal checklist.

The vegetable storeroom was constructed of faded, peeling wooden siding. On the left-hand side stood two tables of bins full of past-sell-by-date vegetables Zachariah collected from several local markets to feed the herbivores. The sickly-sweet stench of overripe peaches filled her nostrils; the vegetables were beginning to rot.

The dry foods section of the storeroom held the mother lode. Bales of hay and alfalfa were stacked in the far corner. Next to them stood the large, one-hundred-gallon vats that contained the grain.

And along all four walls were shelves and shelves heaped full of edible food: canned goods, mostly expired; huge plastic containers of peanut butter, Kodiak's favorite food, especially spread on about three dozen pancakes; commercial-sized boxes of cereal the bonobos loved; special high-fiber biscuit mix for the otters and the black bears; cases of nuts and seeds, bags of popcorn, large bottles of honey to fill the bonobos' and bears' enrichment balls.

She stared at the food, her eyes blurring. Reality struck her with the force of a brick wall. She sagged against the drywall and sank to the floor, her legs no longer able to bear her weight.

Her dad kept a two-week advance store of food. Vlad ate sixty pounds of meat a day. The wolves ate a full deer or calf carcass every three days. The bonobos consumed their weight in fruits, vegetables, and biscuits.

Even if she fed every scrap to the animals, in less than a month, they would starve anyway—Raven along with them.

But all this food for herself alone...she could continue to hunt deer and snare rabbits; could harvest berries, herbs, and other edible plants. Supplemented with what she could scavenge from the forest, this food would last her for well over a year—if she lived, she reminded herself. If she wasn't infected.

A swelling wave of vertigo washed through her. She had that feeling again, like the ground was cracking beneath her, splintering into a gaping, bottomless hole about to swallow her up.

Logically, she knew what she had to do. She needed to choose herself, choose her own survival. Like her mother always insisted when she'd fought with Raven's dad—they were just animals. Thousands of them had probably starved to death in zoos around the country already.

And if Raven was sick, they'd starve without her anyway.

She wouldn't let them starve. That was cruel, inhumane. Her father had asked her to take care of them, to give them mercy. She had access to the tranquilizer guns and the rifles kept in the maintenance shed for emergencies. She could put them down gently, painlessly.

She thought of Vlad. She thought of Suki and Loki, her favorites of the timber wolves. What were the deaths of a few animals in cages compared to the collapse of the civilized world, compared to the catastrophic billions of dead and dying humans?

Only three days ago, she'd been about to turn her back on them permanently. What was different now?

The memory of freshly turned dirt in the woods flashed through her mind. *Only everything.*

Confused and agitated, the bonobos hooted and screeched, calling to each other, escalating into a cacophony of chaos. She closed her eyes.

The guns were in the maintenance shed not fifty feet away. She could go get them now, she could—

Something inside her shriveled. Her mind recoiled from the thought. She'd just buried her father. She wasn't ready. Not yet.

It was better to let them go happily, peacefully, on full stomachs.

She would feed them today. Tomorrow, she would do it. What she'd hadn't summoned the courage to do with her own father. To give mercy.

Tomorrow, she would face every single animal her dad had loved, that she'd grown up with—and end their lives.

9

If Raven had known how the day would end, she would have done several things very differently. But she was still numb with the shock and grief of her father's death. Her only focus was on the tasks at hand, on getting through this endless day, hour by hour, minute by minute.

She had not coughed. She had no fever. But it was early still. The virus simply hadn't made itself known yet. An image of her father flashed through her mind—his bloody tears, face rigid, feverish body contorted in pain.

If that future waited for her, there was nothing she could do to stop it.

She concentrated on putting one foot in front of the other, on the chores she'd completed hundreds of times over the years. She lugged buckets of water from the well just outside the perimeter fence, cleaned each pen, disposed of the manure, and made sure the hay was fresh and not moldy, methodically checking the bottom layers.

It was past noon by the time she loaded up the wagon behind the electric cart for the third time with hay and five-gallon buckets of grain for the herbivores: the deer, the ostriches, Sal the zebra. She'd also managed to fit in a deer carcass for the wolves and cuts of horse meat for the tiger.

She whistled to call Vlad inside his chamber in the tiger house so she could open the gate and give him his food. One long note, two short.

Vlad sauntered to the fence, tail twitching, gazing at her with distinct displeasure at the insult of hunger she'd subjected him to. He turned his rump to her. She jumped back in time to miss the spray of urine.

Vlad's spray had a distinct stink. Zachariah had always said it smelled like hot buttered popcorn. "Hungry?" he'd quip, elbowing her with a grin.

"Very funny," she said to Vlad, blinking hard.

He chuffed at her, making a sound like a throaty cough, obliging and playful again now that he'd adequately punished her.

He was so beautiful, so majestic it made her heart hurt. How incredibly unfair it was to imagine the world without this magnificent creature in it, without any of the animals in it.

She'd spent her life resenting these animals for stealing the time and attention of her father. But she was fond of them, too. More than fond. Her feelings for the animals were a tangled mess, much like her feelings for Haven, her home, and for her father, her mother. In this was the dichotomy of her life—that she simultaneously loved and hated the same things.

"What do you want from me?" she said to the tiger. Then her throat thickened, and she had to finish her work and stride away, fast.

She passed one of the peacocks strolling the grounds, a strutting male who went about pouting and preening, showing off his sapphire-throated elegance and flamboyantly-plumed jewel-green tail feathers. He squawked at her, annoyed.

"I'll get to you," she said as he shimmied his feathers at her.

She decided to cross the grounds out of order to feed the bonobos next. They had been screeching their indignation since yesterday.

The six bonobos lounged in the roped netting strung between three trees inside their habitat; some sleeping, others combing nits from each other's fur. Pepper and Newton chased each other over a tightrope, nimble and sprightly, hands and feet clinging to the rope as they enthusiastically attempted to shake each other off.

Cousins of the chimpanzee, bonobos were the smallest and most intelligent of the apes. Her father had bought them because they were a female-led society, mostly peaceful and less aggressive than chimps. They'd been extinct in the wild for two decades.

Zephyr was the matriarch, the oldest and wisest. She was a patient and calm leader, looking out for the others, breaking up arguments, and protecting her small son Gizmo from the taunts of Pepper and Newton, both four-year-old juveniles. Pepper was particularly calculated and cunning. She would distract the other bonobos and steal their food—especially lettuce, her favorite.

Gizmo bounced on his branch, swinging his arms and offering Raven energetic screeches and hoots. He grinned, his top lip pulled over his teeth, his leathery face relieved and joyful. *Finally*, he seemed to say, *you brought dinner!*

He reached toward her, gesturing with his fingers, his eager, black-licorice eyes gleaming. His black hair was parted in the middle on top of his head, giving him a distinctly human look.

He tugged a grim smile from her. Seeing him so exuberantly

happy made her chest constrict with a hollow ache. "Nice to see you too, Gizmo."

Next were the red foxes. Zoe, Zelda, and Magnus were as energetic as puppies—and almost as tame. One of her favorite things was to go in and rub their bellies and brush the burrs and twigs from their fur and lush red tails.

The Zebra, Sal, was beautiful and vain about keeping the oily black and gleaming white of his coat pristine. But he would sneak up and bite her as soon as her back was turned. He also liked to kick, so she always locked him in his night house when she needed to go inside his pen.

The bobcat, Electra, was ancient at nine years old. She was cute and cuddly-looking with her charming bobbed tail, luxuriously spotted coat, and perky, black-fringed ears, but she had fast reflexes and a predator's instincts. She was still capable of killing a grown man with gruesome efficiency.

Raven's father went right into her pen and scratched her back every day. Electra was known to flip onto her belly and bat playfully —and a little too forcefully—with her razor-sharp claws. Raven's father just shrugged and wrapped whatever scratches she'd left on him.

Or, he used to. He'd never again enter this pen. He'd never again sink to a crouch and crawl around with the wolves or watch Vlad tear into his dinner with serene satisfaction.

Raven sucked in her breath at the memories. She tossed the bobcat the whole, plucked chicken she loved to eat—bones and all. Electra growled appreciatively as she pounced on it.

It was early evening by the time Raven reached the rear of the park, where the wolves reigned over two large, forested enclosures. The first enclosure was the largest, and held the six timber wolves. Behind a tall chain-link fence topped with electrified wires, the wolves prowled through a copse of trees in the center of their enclosure.

She knew these wolves the best of all the animals. Because they were her father's favorites, they were hers as well. She remembered long, sweltering afternoons of hunkering down before the fence to watch her father inside the enclosure with the wolves.

He would sit with them, frolic with them, sleep with them. It had taken months of patience, but little by little, the pack had accepted him. Raven had watched it happen with a bitter mix of envy, awe, resentment, admiration.

Normally shy and wary, the wolves usually kept to the cover of the trees during the day. But they knew her scent and the smell of food. One by one, they appeared between the trees and drifted into the clearing a few dozen yards from the double-fence line.

Titus and Loki were the closest, Loki coming right up to the fence, tongue lolling, ears pricked. Loki, god of mischief, was aptly named. He was the smallest of the wolves, but made up for it in abundant energy. Curious and mischievous, he always had a spring to his step, was always the first awake and ready to play. He was the first to come to her father when he started spending time inside their paddock.

Titus stood tense, ears pricked, fur raised, tail stiff behind him. Not aggressive, but protective. He was the beta. Four years old and in his prime, he was a bruiser; tall, thick-chested and bulky. The beta was the bouncer of the pack, the alphas' enforcer, the first to snap at any wolf out of line.

"I've brought dinner," she said.

Suki whined eagerly and took a tentative step forward, her tail lifting. She was the shyest wolf and the youngest, a yearling. Suki was sweet and gentle, the peacekeeper, the one who always broke up arguments before Titus or Aspen had to get involved.

Her name was Japanese for "beloved." Her dad named her when he nursed her from a pup after a she-wolf from another zoo had rejected her young. It was the only sentimental thing Raven had ever seen him do.

The last three wolves hung back.

Echo was spindly, with a straggly, uneven grey coat, a chunk bitten out of his right ear, and a perpetual slinking manner, an air of cowardice. He was the omega, the lowest wolf on the totem pole.

The other two were the alpha pair, Shika and Aspen. A brindled she-wolf, Shika came to them unnamed, so Raven's dad gave her the Japanese name that meant "as a deer," fleet-footed. She had a savage, restless beauty about her. And she was fast, easily outpacing her lifemate, Aspen.

Aspen was six years old, with a magnificent shaggy ruff and a single dark stripe down the center of his muzzle. He stood close to Shika, both of their yellow eyes fixed on Raven.

The alpha wolf wasn't the bold, aggressive, take-charge type like most people thought. That was the role of the beta, the alpha's second-in-command. The alpha was the brains behind the operation, the central nervous system that kept the pack together and working properly. The alpha was wary, cautious; he protected himself and the critical, hard-won knowledge and experience that kept his family alive.

The male never led alone; it was a partnership, like the parents of a family. That was pack.

After she'd lured the wolves to their den, Raven hauled the deer carcass from the wagon and dumped it in their enclosure. In the wild, wolf hierarchy was established by who ate what, so her father preferred to feed the wolves a whole carcass instead of joints of meat. Sometimes they fed the wolves a calf carcass, but her dad liked to hunt deer when he could instead of purchasing meat from the slaughterhouse or renderer.

Memories lay thick and heavy over every inch of this place. Everywhere she looked, she could see him: lounging beneath the sprawling oak with the wolves; striding along the flagstone pathways, trailed by a peacock or two; bent over the fences, checking for breaches; driving the electric cart everywhere, hauling water and food and hay.

Her chest tightened. For a moment, it was hard to breathe. She pushed the feelings away. She had too much to do to waste time feeling sorry for herself.

She released the wolves to their dinner.

It was a bizarre and sometimes frightening thing to watch wolves eat. They snapped and snarled at each other, fangs bared in a frenzy of furious excitement. If one tried to take a bite from a section that wasn't theirs, the other wolves growled and bit at him.

It seemed savage from the outside, but her father had explained that the higher-ranking wolves were giving lessons, teaching the lower wolves, ensuring every wolf remembered their place in the pack.

A wolf pack used food as a way to maintain order. Each wolf had a spot—prized organs, neck, flank—earned depending on its rank and role within the pack. The meat they ate affected the distinctive smell of their urine, which they used to signal identity, status, and role.

Her dad had told her once of a pack in the wild whose natural prey had been so depleted, they'd been forced to catch salmon from the river. With every wolf eating the same thing, their urine lost their markers. Each individual wolf lost its identity. The pack descended into chaos and collapsed.

The sun was sinking below the treeline by the time Raven

moved on to the next enclosure. She was tired, her arms aching, her belly rumbling, but she forced herself to keep moving. As long as there was work to do, she could force out the pain, the memories, the hovering darkness threatening to devour her the second she let her guard down.

This was also a wolf enclosure, but these wolves were kept separate from the timber wolves. They were too dangerous.

Her father was adamant that Haven only house real wild animals; he'd refused the genetically modified exotic animals most zoos used now. Called mods, they were engineered to be meek and docile.

By law, scientists were required to ensure the mods didn't breed, and only very specific, qualified companies were allowed to create mods. But as always, a black market sprang up, driven by the elites' desire to acquire the most exotic pets to accentuate their chic designer outfits and fabulous mansions.

There were those who desired the size and strength of a mod, but with extras for certain nefarious activities. Both wolves had been rescued last year from an underground exotic animal fighting ring. To gain the advantage in the ring, their owners had illegally bred them to produce a hybrid with the size of a mod and the cunning intelligence of the wild-born wolf.

No other zoo or refuge in the area had been willing to take them. Finally, her father had relented, and they were brought to Haven.

"Stay away from them," her father had cautioned. He had never warned her about any other animal in the park—not Kodiak, not Titus, not Vlad.

No one went inside this enclosure other than Dad. Last summer, Zachariah's teenage nephew was sent to the hospital after he reached through the chain-link to scratch Luna when she rubbed her back against the fence. Luna had whipped around and chomped down on two of his fingers. He almost lost them both.

Zachariah had warned him, but the boy thought he knew better. Wolves weren't dogs. And hybrids weren't even wolves. They were some nebulous *other*—beautiful but terrifying.

Raven stepped up to the fence, peering through the maple, elm, and ash trees, searching the shifting shadows. She felt their presence, knew they were watching. They were always watching.

"Come out now," she said softly.

Luna appeared like a ghost between two trees at the rear of the enclosure. She was huge, easily over two hundred pounds, her coat as pure white as driven snow. Standing still, her amber eyes fixed on Raven like she could see straight through her.

A shadow separated from the deeper shadows beneath the trees, forming into an enormous wolf, this one the ink-black of a night devoid of stars. His broad shoulders and chest rippled with muscles beneath his thick fur.

The black wolf raised his regal head, his muzzle long and narrow, his gaze intelligent, cunning. He'd been named Shadow for the way he seemed to merge with the darkness, appearing and disappearing at will.

For a long moment, the hybrid wolves stared at her, and she, at them.

Abruptly, Luna's ears flattened against her skull. Her eyes slitted and she growled, her jowls pulled back to reveal sharp, gleaming teeth.

Shadow snarled, hackles raised, tail stiff behind him.

The hairs on Raven's arms stood on end. Instinctively, she stepped back, fear surging through her. Logically, she knew there was a double fence between them, that she was safe, but her brain buzzed with alarm, screaming that two enormous predators were intent on devouring her.

Both wolves growled savagely, their jaws snapping, backs arched, hackles bristling. Raven took another step back. "Easy now. Just calm down for a second—"

That was when she heard it.

The rumble of motorcycles.

10

It took Raven a moment to place the sound. She hadn't heard a car out here in almost a month. Even then, almost every vehicle on the road was electric. The motorcycles were aggressively loud, their unmuffled engines revving, crashing through the stillness like thunder.

She stilled, rooted in place. Her mind whirred with terrible possibility after terrible possibility, each one worse than the last. They could be looters or vandals, criminals or serial killers.

She already knew who they were—the bikers from Clay Creek, from the pharmacy.

But what the heck were they doing here?

She couldn't stick around to find out. She fought off the panic closing around her throat. She wasn't sure what to do, but standing here, waiting like a sitting duck, was a monumentally bad idea.

Maybe she could hide in the crawl space beneath the lodge, wait it out until they left. She couldn't head for the car—it was in the parking lot, right where the bikers were headed. Besides, it was uncharged.

Maybe she should just flee like she'd planned all along, make a run for it. Though her pack with her supplies was in her bedroom in the lodge. She needed the supplies in that pack to survive alone for days in the woods. She couldn't run without it.

Maybe she should find a weapon, prepare to defend Haven and herself from whatever these thugs planned to do. The maintenance shed was located between the lodge and the food prep buildings on the northeast side of the park. The tranquilizers were kept in there. And her father's guns.

Either way—run, hide, or fight—she had to go the same direction: toward the oncoming motorcycles. The evening light was fading fast, the sky deepening to indigo, crickets beginning their night songs, but it was still bright enough to see clearly. No matter what she did, right now she had to get herself out of sight.

Raven broke into a run. She turned and sprinted left, abandoning the exposed flagstone path for a worn-in trail through the weeds and bric-a-brac behind the exhibits. At the back end of the park, she had to race past the bears, the ostrich pen, the smaller porcupine, eagle, and otter exhibits, the bonobos' house, and finally the reptile house to reach the storage buildings nestled out of the public's sight behind a screen of poplar, oak, and maple trees.

The motorcycles grew louder. They were still obscured by the trees. A nine-mile gravel road winding through heavy forest brought visitors to the main parking lot and the front entrance, which was gated—and locked.

At best, it would only slow intruders down. Though electrified top wires were strung along the exterior perimeter, the wrought-iron fence was more for looks—and keeping wild creatures in—than protection from outside threats.

The gates wouldn't deter them for long.

Even inside the grounds, there was plenty of foliage to shield her as she raced between the storage buildings. Her father had insisted the park keep as many of the natural trees and bushes on the property as they could. She hesitated for a moment before bypassing the maintenance shed.

A gun didn't seem like a good idea. She knew how to use one, had hunted deer with her father dozens of times, but this was entirely different. She wouldn't stand a chance against a gang of experienced, strong, violent fighters.

The motorcycles roared into the parking lot. The engines switched off. Loud, raucous voices filled the air with shouts and jeers and curses.

She pressed herself against the rear wall of the lodge. Her pulse thudded against her throat. *Run.* She needed to grab her gear and escape to the woods.

Except that her window was located on the west side of the building, directly in the line of sight of the bikers. And the ground dipped along the rear of the lodge, making the back windows—a bathroom, her father's room, a guest bedroom—over ten feet from the ground. There were no nearby trees, no way to reach them.

She needed a plan B, whatever that was.

She eased around the corner, cautiously scanning the front of the park. She counted ten bikers gathered outside the gates, including the ones from the pharmacy. She recognized several: burly, blond Scorpio; Damien with the sharp fox-face and the piercings; Ryker, the dead-eyed one who'd shot Carl in the face. And the gaunt, pony-tailed one, whose name she didn't know.

Of the half-dozen bikers she didn't recognize, one stood out— partly because he stood at least half a head taller than the others. He was huge, with a barrel of a chest and blue tattoos squirming across his bulging arms. She was close enough to make out his square, stubbled jaw and chestnut-brown hair shorn close to his skull. He sauntered up to the gates with one hand on his rifle butt, his shrewd gaze assessing everything as he scanned his surroundings.

The others blended together—tough, brawny, terrifying. They carried various weapons—rifles, knives, and guns. Most wore gloves, with masks tugged down around their necks. And they all circled around the tall man, waiting on his orders. He was clearly their leader. This one must be Cerberus, the name Scorpio had mentioned at the pharmacy.

She strained to make out their voices.

Ponytail scratched his scalp. "What the hell is this place?"

"A wildlife refuge," Damien said, reading the sign affixed to the gates. Ponytail looked at him blankly. "Like a private zoo."

"The animals are probably already dead," Scorpio said. "Or else those crazy Earth Liberation activists released them, like they did in Atlanta."

Kodiak, the black bear, gave a half-hearted bellow.

Cerberus threw back his head and laughed. "Do you hear that?"

"That a lion?" asked a heavy, bearded Middle Eastern man, his beady eyes going wide.

"You're an idiot, Oman," Damien said. "Don't you recognize a bear when you hear one?"

Oman scowled, but Ryker and Scorpio laughed. Damien's face flushed at the show of approval.

"What a pleasant surprise," Cerberus said, peering through the bars of the gate and taking in the restaurant, the lodge, the picnic tables, the souvenir shop designed like a log cabin. "A precious jewel hidden away in the middle of nowhere."

The tiger's roar punctuated the quiet evening air.

The bikers froze and stared at each other, gaping in startled awe.

Vlad roared again and again, the deep bass notes ringing across the grounds. It was a frightening and awe-inspiring thing, conjuring an image of something enormous, vicious, and very hungry.

A savage grin spreading across his face, Cerberus slapped Damien on the back so hard he stumbled. "Gentlemen, we've just entered the jungle. Happy hunting."

"What about the girl?" Ryker asked, sounding bored.

Raven stiffened. Ryker had seen her, noticed her, stared at her like she was prey. He and the others must have decided to find her. She'd been so intent on getting home, so shaken from the shooting, that she wouldn't have noticed if one of them had hitched a ride in the back seat of her battered Toyota.

"She might be here; she might not," Scorpio said. "How much time do you want to waste looking for her?"

"She's here." Ryker scanned the trees as he prowled next to Cerberus, hand resting on his holster. He was probably Cerberus's beta, his enforcer. Ryker pointed toward the carport at the other end of the parking lot. "That's her car."

"If you find her, bring her to me," Cerberus said. "I have a particular client who would...appreciate her exotic flair."

Raven sucked in her breath, her face flushing hot in anger. They could go to hell. Every single one of them. They were murderers and worse. She'd make sure they never found her.

"I think we'll get something out of this place," Cerberus said, still grinning broadly. "Let's have a look around before it gets too dark. We'll stay here for the night."

"How about something edible?" Ponytail said. His voice was deep and rough, like gravel. "I'm starving."

Oman sniggered. "Don't accidentally walk into the bear cage, Jagger, or you'll be edible."

Oman flashed an ingratiating smile at Cerberus, gauging his

reaction. Cerberus ignored him. Beside him, Ryker sneered down at Oman dismissively. Oman slunk several paces away.

There was a hierarchy among the bikers, with the same jostling for power and dominance as a wolf pack. In this case, she doubted the alpha treated his pack like family.

"Gentlemen, a treat just landed right in our laps," Cerberus bellowed, gathering the men around him. "Let's go see just how sweet it is."

Oman grabbed the bars of the gate and rattled them. "How we gettin' inside, boss?"

Jagger narrowed his eyes at the bioscan lock. "No way to hack this."

"Grab the hook," Cerberus ordered. "And the chains."

"What are you waiting for?" Ryker clapped his hands. "Get to it."

Raven watched in growing dread as several bikers jogged back to their motorcycles, one pulling a large metal hook and chains from a case attached to the rear of the bike. Jagger grabbed what looked like a bolt cutter and went to work on the gates' hinges.

Oman and Damien wrapped the chains around the gate, attached them to the rear of several bikes, and pulled away with a squeal of tires and revving engines. The gate wrenched off its snapped hinges with a sickening shriek of metal.

The bikers strode through the opened gates like they already owned the place. Cerberus turned to Damien, Jagger, and a third guy—a slight, stoop-shouldered Latino in his forties, wearing a khaki jacket too large for him and a dirty brown baseball cap pulled low over his forehead. "Damien, find us a place to sleep. Jagger and Gomez, you're on food patrol. Scrounge up something decent to eat."

Damien nodded sharply, and the bikers began to disperse,

laughing and conversing among themselves. Jagger and the Latino guy—Gomez—headed toward the lodge, directly toward Raven's hiding spot. Three more found the main path, flicked their Smart-Flexes, and activated the flashlight feature as dusk thickened around them.

She had to move. Now.

She was grateful for the growing darkness. She knew the layout of this place like the back of her hand. The dark would give her a slight advantage—an advantage she'd need if she was going to survive the night.

11

Raven rose cautiously to her feet and backed slowly away.

Like all predators, rapid movement would attract their attention and trigger their prey-response. If she stayed quiet and hidden, she could creep behind the buildings, head to the back of the park, reach the rear gate, and escape into the woods.

She had no food or water or shelter—she wouldn't last long. But a single night while these thugs took what they wanted and then went on their merry way—that was doable. They'd take some of the food, but there were only ten of them.

There would still be enough for her. There would have to be enough.

She didn't have many options, anyway. This was the best she could think of.

The sky was nearly black now, stars winking to life overhead. Thick clouds drifted like ribbons across the moon. Without electricity, the automatic security lights strung along the pathways were dark.

Moving carefully within the shadows, she managed to reach the maintenance shed without detection. The air had grown chilly. A glance at her dad's SmartFlex told her it was forty-eight degrees and dropping. She didn't feel it now, but would later, alone in the woods in the middle of a cold fall night.

She crouched, eyeing the ten yards of open ground she had to cross to reach the cover of the thin line of trees between the shed and the food storage buildings. Once she reached the trees, she'd be invisible.

Three men rounded the corner of the lodge, coming toward her from the far side, their flashlights sweeping the ground along the wrought-iron fence. She blinked against the brightness, unable to make out their features, only their vaguely human shapes.

She cringed back against the wall. They were between her and the fence. As soon as they reached the shed, they'd find her.

She cursed silently. Still crouching, she crept along the rear of the shed and peeked around the opposite corner. She was facing the park now. On her left clustered the lodge, the restaurant, the souvenir shop, and the entrance. There were men bumbling around inside the restaurant, more exploring the lodge—her *home*. They had no right to invade that private space. She shoved that thought out of her mind. There was no time.

To the right, the flagstone path led past the food storage buildings to the eastern exhibits: the reptile house, the bonobos, the otters, eagle, and porcupines, the ostriches, then finally the bears and wolves at the rear.

Maybe, just maybe, she would get lucky, and the thugs investigating the park had chosen the western path instead of the east one closest to her. If they had, they would be all the way on the far side, the large lake and walk-in enclosure between her and them.

She had only a second to make the decision. The goons behind her would discover her position within moments. She inched out from behind the maintenance shed and moved to the path. It was lined with waist-high bushes, slim birch trees interspersed every thirty feet or so. Other than the bushes, there wasn't much to provide cover until she reached the reptile house another fifty yards away.

She needed to hurry.

Raven ducked behind the bushes along the path and crawled on her hands and knees. Twigs and burrs jabbed into her palms. The woodsy scent of mulch filled her nostrils.

Voices rang out behind her. Harsh, braying laughter echoed. Flashlight beams swept across the darkened sky.

She crawled faster. Despite the cold, sweat beaded her forehead. She focused on the next step to drive away the icy shock of panic trembling her limbs. Get out of sight. Get to the rear gate. *Get out. Get out. Get out.*

She rose, splinters of mulch needling her kneecaps, and peered cautiously over the hedge. The shadowy bulk of the reptile house reared up out of the night.

She dropped back down and kept crawling. When she checked again, she'd reached the eagle house. She could just make out the shape of Hera, the American bald eagle, napping on a high branch within the mesh walls.

It was frustratingly slow going. Every time she lowered her knee, she winced, the soft crunching sound loud as an explosion in her ears. She sucked in her breath between her teeth to keep from gasping.

Finally, she reached the bears. The wrought-iron perimeter fence was only a few yards behind the bear and wolf exhibits. She strained for strange noises over the trill of insects, a peacock squawking, and the squealing of the bonobos across the park.

Voices. Not too close yet, but closing in. A flashlight beam bobbed behind her. Danger headed her way.

Slowly, heart thudding, she rose to her feet.

The bear enclosure was large. To circle around to the back, she was first forced to walk along a section of path directly in front of the enclosure about twenty yards long. It was devoid of topiary bushes, leaving her exposed.

Her boots scuffed the flagstone. She softened her footfalls. Her eyes strained in the dim moonlight, constantly scanning, searching for danger, for anything—

A shadow that didn't belong.

Directly ahead of her, a large shape bent over the railing of the bear habitat, completely still and unmoving in the darkness.

She blinked. It was still there. Her eyes adjusted enough to recognize that the shape was distinctly human.

Adrenaline shot through her veins. She stifled a cry of alarm.

She couldn't turn and go back the way she'd come. There were bikers behind her. Raven did the only thing she could think of. She took off running.

As she raced past the bear enclosure, the shadow moved, jerking back, startled. "Hey!" he said. "Hey! Stop!"

His footfalls slapped the flagstone behind her. He cursed, fumbling with something, probably trying to activate a flashlight.

Her pursuer was larger than she was. Stronger. Likely faster. She wouldn't be able to outrun him. Her only chance was to hide— to hide where he was least likely to look.

There weren't many options.

It was a risk. It was dangerous. But between human predators who she'd already seen kill and animal predators who rarely or never killed humans in the wild…it wasn't even a choice.

Raven wheeled sharply and fled between the enclosures.

The timber wolf paddock was surrounded by a double-fence. She pressed her shaking right hand to the bioscanner, opened the outside gate, slipped inside, and relocked it. She sprinted to the inside gate, opened it, and entered, willing her limbs to stop shaking, willing herself to calm the hell down.

Wolves could smell fear. They knew if your heart rate increased, could scent every molecule of your sour, panicked sweat.

She not only couldn't show her fear, she couldn't allow herself to feel it, either.

She took one deep, steadying breath. *Crouch low at their level and don't move,* her dad had instructed the few times he'd brought her inside the fence. *Don't startle them. Show you're submissive. Speak in their language.*

On the path behind her, a flashlight beam flickered to life.

There was no time. She was exposed. At any second, the thug would discover her. She had to get out of the clearing into the small forested area around the perimeter. She had to move, to hide—right freakin' now.

It was only then, in the almost pitch darkness, her heart hammering against her ribs, that she realized.

The deer carcass she'd fed to the timber wolves hours before was missing.

It had been right here, not twenty yards in. The wolves wouldn't have finished the carcass yet. And even if they had, there would be bones, a skull, patches of fur, gristle.

Raven went perfectly still. Her heart turned to ice in her chest.

The timber wolves' deer carcass wasn't here because she wasn't inside the timber wolves' enclosure. In her panic, she'd entered the second enclosure instead.

She'd just locked herself in with the hybrid wolves.

12

S weat beaded beneath Raven's armpits, along the inside of her knees. Her breath came in sharp, shallow gasps.

These were not the timber wolves she knew and understood. Still deadly, still dangerous. But at least *familiar*.

The hybrid wolves were completely *other*.

Raven almost turned around. She almost lost her nerve and fled back to the gate.

The beam of the flashlight swept across a copse of trees a dozen yards to her right. Fear surged through her. Her pursuer was still searching for her.

Killer humans or killer wolves. It was a terrible choice. Still, in that moment, she was more afraid of the killer humans.

Frantic, she searched for a hiding spot within the enclosure—a wide oak trunk, a thick bush, a fallen log—anything. She squinted, peering into the darkness, a darkness that held any number of monsters.

She scrambled down the shallow incline, shoved brambles and underbrush aside, and dove behind the trunk of a hickory tree. The bark scraped her back as she pressed against it, but she hardly noticed.

The flashlight skimmed over her hiding place. The light glinted off something in the brush deeper in the trees. The light stilled on a spot directly ahead of her, not five yards from where she huddled behind the trunk.

Two pairs of reflective eyes peered back at her.

Raven went very still.

The biker still on the path above her kept the flashlight beam trained on the twin pairs of glowing eyes. He swore softly. He saw them, too.

She glimpsed a halo of white among the darkly gleaming leaves. It was Luna. Luna's mate remained utterly camouflaged in the darkness; Raven saw only the glittering eyes staring intently back at her.

Every hair on the back of her neck stood on end.

She was trapped inside a cage with two genetically modified wolves almost twice her weight, designed by nature and man to maim and kill with impunity, with a bite force of fifteen hundred pounds per square inch.

It took every ounce of courage not to scream. She gritted her teeth, her muscles taut and thrumming with panic-spiked adrenaline, counting the eternal seconds until the flashlight finally swept away.

Luna's ears twitched as the biker stumbled down the path away from the enclosure, the flashlight wavering wildly. The wolf never took her gaze off Raven.

Raven immediately dropped her gaze in submission. It seemed like the wolves stared at her forever. Were they taking her measure? Did they see her as a potential threat? Or were they deciding which parts of her to eat first? She knew that answer. Her organs. Her heart, lungs, stomach, intestines. Alphas always got the choicest bits...

Her stomach lurched. She couldn't think like that, couldn't resign herself to a fate not set in stone. Not until they tore out her warm, still-beating heart.

In an eye blink, the wolves vanished. It was that fast. One second, they were there. The next, they'd faded silently into the darkness.

She peered into the gloom, her gaze sweeping from left to right and left again, straining to make out a familiar predatory shape in the shadows. She'd thought it couldn't get worse. But it could. Not seeing them, not having any idea where they were, whether they were sneaking up on her right this second, preparing to pounce from any direction—this was worse.

Could she leave? Had they grown tired of her and wandered off somewhere to sleep? Maybe she could rise cautiously and sneak back to the gate...

But no. There would be no sneaking. Not with wolves. They could detect her every movement by scent. They would know the second she stood.

If she made it to the fence, it would only be because they'd allowed it, as opposed to ambushing her and ripping her throat out.

It was worth a chance. Better than sitting here and waiting for death to come to her. Slowly, slowly, she rose from her crouch. Something sharp jabbed into her thigh. Adrenaline shot through her —images of gleaming claws and fangs flashing through her mind— until she realized what it was.

Her whittling knife, still in her pocket because she hadn't changed since yesterday, since she'd buried her dad.

Raven drew it from her pocket and flipped out the three-inch blade. It wasn't much. But it was better than nothing.

She took a single cautious step. Dead leaves crackled beneath her boot.

A low growl erupted from the bushes directly ahead of her.

Raven froze.

The black wolf materialized out of the darkness.

She forgot how to breathe.

He stood between two slim maple trees less than ten feet from her, stiff-legged, tail straight out behind him. He tilted his regal head, studying her with those intense, probing eyes.

He growled again, ears flattening.

Instinctively, she backed up against the tree and lowered herself, so she was smaller than he was, less of a threat. She gripped the knife but kept it low and pressed against her thigh.

"Whoa now," she said softly. "I'm not here to hurt you."

As soon as she sat back down, the wolf's ears lifted. He gave her a piercing look, as if to say, *now stay there.*

She settled against the ridged, furrowed bark of the hickory tree, yellowed leaves rustling over her head. "You want me right here where you can keep an eye on me," she murmured, still hardly daring to breathe. "Is that it?"

Shadow prowled in a slow, languid circle around her, sniffing the ground, the air, never breaching that ten-foot radius. Ten feet or ten inches, it hardly mattered. His jaws could snap around her throat in less than a second if he wished.

After five minutes of circling while Raven sat rigid, nearly passing out from lack of oxygen, the wolf loped away, disappearing into the underbrush.

This time she knew better than to move. He was still there, just out of sight, watching her. Both of the wolves were there. She could feel their presence in the prickling of her skin, the rapid beat of her heart.

This was their territory. She was the intruder. Whether she lived or died tonight was entirely up to them.

She inhaled a slow, shaky breath and glanced up. Should she try to climb the tree, escape their reach? But there were no low branches. She scanned the other trees—all too slim to bear her weight, or the branches began too high. Besides, movement would attract the wolves. They'd be on her in a heartbeat if they deemed her actions threatening in any way.

She sat against the tree trunk and waited, the knife clenched at her side. There was nothing else for her to do. The cold ground seeped through her pants and chilled her legs and backside. Above her head, the sickle of a moon hung in the trees, caught in a snarl of branches.

She listened to the heartbeat of the night, the pitter-patter of tiny nocturnal creatures, the soughing of the wind through the trees. She strained for any sound or glimpse of the wolves, but there was nothing. They moved through the darkness like ghosts.

An hour later, the black wolf returned.

13

This time, the wolf came far closer.

He trotted around Raven, sniffing the ground. He circled her again and again, each time closer, closer.

She waited and watched, forcing herself to breathe, to keep her heart from hammering right out of her chest. *Don't be afraid, don't be afraid. Don't give him a reason to kill you.*

His behavior was much like the timber wolves investigating some new toy or strange object in their enclosure. Almost like a dog.

But he was no dog. He was enormous. This close, she had to look up at him. His high, regal head, long muzzle, and sharp, inquisitive eyes gleaming with intelligence. That broad, thickly furred chest and long, lean legs.

He bounded close to sniff at the soles of her boots. She gasped, her brain shrieking in alarm. Just as quickly, he darted away.

Shadow half-turned as if to leave. Then suddenly, without warning, he whirled on her. He snapped his jaws and nipped her shoulder.

She flinched, stunned. *Run!* Her brain screamed at her.

But her brain was a liar. To run now would trigger his prey-response. Instinct would drive him to attack, even if that wasn't his original intention.

She couldn't run. She couldn't do anything but remain statue-still and endure this.

Her shoulder smarted. Slowly, gingerly, she felt it. No blood. No missing chunks of flesh.

The wolf hadn't bitten her. He wasn't trying to hurt her. Or at least, not much. Not yet.

He was interested in something else.

Shadow disappeared into the underbrush. Again, Raven waited.

Another hour passed. The air grew colder and colder. Slender white-trunked birch trees glowed faintly in the moonlight. Sticks and branches littered the ground at her feet.

To keep herself awake, she reached out and picked up a stick, thick as her forearm, about a foot long. It was a good stick for whittling.

At least she still had the knife. An image of the blood-streaked wooden bird she'd carved at her father's bedside flitted through her mind. She pushed it out. She couldn't think of that now—her father's body stiffening, growing cold, the red Georgia clay filling his gaping mouth, pressing against his dead eyes.

She scraped off the bark in sharp, jerky movements. She inhaled a breath. *Focus.* Drive every bad thought out. She forced herself to be calm—at least as calm as could be expected in her situation—trapped inside a cage with killer wolves, killer men roaming outside it, waiting to strike.

She made long, sweeping cuts with the grain, carving a rough outline, breathing deep with each stroke. Her hands fell back into the familiar rhythm almost without purposeful thought. Using push and pull cuts, she gently carved the soft shape, the curve of the body, the sweep of the wings, the arc of the head and sharp V of the beak.

Another hour passed. Wood shavings scattered in the leaves beneath her. She smiled grimly down at the little raven, cradling it in her palm, an ache in her chest. She used to leave them around the house for her mother and father both. Only her mother ever noticed them, tucked in her dresser drawer or nestled beneath her pillow.

To her father, they were useless, for they served no purpose. She remembered the punch-in-the-gut feeling the first time he'd swept one into the trash. "Carve a walking stick or a knife handle," he'd said, already striding toward the door, off to another chore, yet another task. "Something worthwhile."

How Raven missed them now—both of them—even as she resented them for leaving her behind, abandoned and completely alone, trapped in a nightmare that wouldn't end.

She'd thought being alone was what she wanted. She was wrong.

The truth was, no matter how much she'd tried to hate her mother, no matter how thick the thorns of resentment and anger had grown around her heart, Raven could not stop loving her. And the loving hurt more than hate ever could.

Because in the end, her mother hadn't loved her enough to come back.

Raven placed the bird carving on the cold, leaf-strewn ground. She blinked rapidly, fighting back the stinging in her eyes. She didn't cry. She never cried. Tears were weakness, her father always said— used to say.

A small moan escaped her lips. She shouldn't think of these things, shouldn't feel the pain twisting inside her ribs. Not now, when she had to focus every fiber of her being on survival.

She drew her knees up to her chest, shivering, and concentrating on the night sounds. A symphony of crickets. The low haunting hoot of an owl. The skitter of a small creature through the leaves.

Despite the danger, her exhaustion caught up to her. She'd barely slept in three days. More than once, she dozed off, jerking awake with a start at every rustle in the brush, every cracking twig.

She felt, rather than heard, the wolf's return.

Her eyes snapped open.

Shadow stood less than four feet away. He was staring at her.

He sprang in close, nipping her knee. His fangs ripped a small hole in her pants, scraping against her skin.

Her eyes stung at the sudden pain. She didn't move.

He was so close the damp musk of his coat filled her nostrils. Hot breath streamed between his opened jaws, pink tongue lolling. Mud coated the bottom of his gigantic paws.

He stood over her, lowered his head, and nipped her calf.

She swallowed a whimper.

He gave her a calculating, inscrutable look, as if he were searching for something. His amber gaze was penetrating, like he was staring right through her, could see every beat of her shuddering heart. A strange, wondrous terror filled her.

Shadow stepped to the side, across her legs, and bumped hard against her shoulder as he passed. He would have knocked her over without the trunk braced at her back.

He circled so close he brushed against her with every turn. His body was solid, all corded muscle, coiled strength and power. His fur was wiry, coarse, and thick.

He didn't want to hurt her. He was investigating her, making sure she wasn't a threat—but also checking if she were something he'd enjoy devouring. Each time he brushed against her and she didn't act like prey or predator, it strengthened his decision to let her be.

Relief cascaded through her. Shadow would let her go. The relief lasted only an instant.

Shadow spun so swiftly her brain barely registered it. He lunged in and snapped, growling deep in his throat, lips curled back from his teeth.

He snarled inches from her face. A spray of saliva struck her cheeks. His hot, wet breath seared her skin.

Terror stopped her breath.

The wolf seized her neck in his jaws.

14

Raven froze. Not swallowing, not breathing, not moving a millimeter.

The wolf's teeth pricked the flesh over her jugular. His powerful jaws, barely tightened, would pulverize her neck, her spine, and crush the breath from her body.

He could kill her in a heartbeat without even meaning to.

She considered stabbing him with the whittling knife, but that would cause him to bite instinctively. Either way, she was dead.

She was completely helpless. There was nothing she could do but remain still and count the eternal seconds in her mind, willing herself not to panic, to lock her terror somewhere deep inside.

Five seconds passed. Ten. Twenty. Forty-five.

Finally, the wolf released her throat.

She gasped for breath, desperately sucking in oxygen. Still, she kept herself completely motionless. She felt a single bead of blood snake down the side of her neck.

The wolf stepped back and stared at her with his yellow eyes.

He didn't growl or yelp or bare his teeth. He simply watched her, shrewd, assessing.

What was she supposed to do now? He wanted something. Expected her to do something. But what?

Her mind raced, scrolling back through her conversations and observations of her father, all the things he'd taught her about wolf biology and behavior.

It was a test.

This whole night was a test, from the circling to bumping into her to nipping her shoulder and leg. By seizing her neck—one of the most vulnerable parts of the body—he was displaying his power and authority as alpha. He was demonstrating his ability to kill her if he wished.

She had to prove that she understood him. Immediately, she dropped her knife and rolled onto her back, exposing her belly in submission, showing him she knew how absolutely defenseless she was, proving she recognized he was the one with the power. It was a request for trust.

Trust being the one thing she was horrible at.

"You can trust me," she whispered. "You're in charge. I respect you as the leader above me."

Again, he took her throat in his jaws.

She lay there, every muscle taut, staring glassy-eyed at the patches of star-spangled sky through the black branches.

Her heart beat in her throat, pulsing against his jaws.

He squeezed her neck harder. *You know what I am capable of,* he seemed to say. He was purposefully choosing not to harm her, proving that she could trust him back.

"I understand," she forced out.

He let go of her neck and stepped back.

He watched as she pulled herself to a sitting position, breathing hard. She rubbed her throat. It was tender, slick with hot saliva, but apart from the single, shallow puncture, she was unharmed.

Relief and astonished awe filled her. He could have killed her, but he didn't. A true alpha wasn't the one who used brute force. He was the one who chose not to.

"Thank you," she whispered. "Thank you."

His ears flicked, and his tail wagged gently.

Shadow trotted away, then paused and glanced back over his shoulder. An invitation. He wanted her to follow him.

She did.

Raven fumbled through the leaves, found her knife, closed it, and shoved it and the carving in her cargo pocket. She rose to her feet, not bothering to comb the leaves from her hair or brush the dirt from her pants.

Her heart pumping, a sharp, wild-edged thrill thrumming through every cell in her body, she followed the wolf through the trees and thick underbrush. He led her to the far right side of the enclosure, where the wolf den, the night house, was located.

She broke into the small clearing and halted.

The white she-wolf, Luna, lurked at the edge of the den entrance. Her hackles lifted, her lips peeling back in a growl. Not fearful, but wary.

Luna was the distrustful one. That made her smart. People could whisper *I love you* and *I miss you* while stabbing you in the back. Raven knew that better than most.

She lifted her hands, palms out in a gesture of surrender, and took a step back. Luna's growl deepened.

Of course. A wolf wouldn't understand human gestures of surrender. Raven dropped to a hunched sitting position, making herself small and submissive. "I'm not a threat to you. I promise."

Luna turned her growl on Shadow. He wagged his tail at her.

She showed her teeth, reiterating her displeasure at Raven's presence, clearly an interloper who didn't belong.

He licked her muzzle, ears pricked hopefully. She snapped at him and sashayed out of reach.

Undaunted, Shadow loped to her and nuzzled her side softly. Her lips pulled back. She gave him a severe, disapproving look before snapping again.

This time, Shadow backed off with a low whimper.

Luna turned and stalked into the den, hackles raised and growling, abandoning Shadow and Raven to the cold.

"She's mad at you," Raven said. "I think she would have preferred me for dinner."

Shadow's ears and tail drooped in disappointment. He knew rejection when he saw it.

"You and me both," she dared to whisper.

Shadow rubbed against Raven's side with a whine, nearly knocking her over again. He circled a few times and flopped to the ground, stretching out beside Raven, so close that she could feel the heat radiating from his large body.

She listened to the sound of his easy, contented panting. She didn't dare touch him, though she wanted to. She simply watched him, awestruck.

The whole insane night filled her with a marvelous incredulity, fascination, and reverence, along with a host of inexplicable emotions she couldn't name, let alone describe.

This was what her dad must have felt all those years, so close to the wild creatures he'd loved. It was like she was connected to some hidden, unseen thing greater than herself, united in this moment with the vast, unknowable universe.

Like she'd just touched a dazzling star with her bare hands.

She had not forgotten the danger the bikers posed. She had not forgotten that her father was dead, that her mother had abandoned her, or that the Hydra virus might be proliferating inside her right now, hijacking her cells and turning her own body traitor against her.

She had not forgotten that outside Haven's wrought-iron walls, the world was descending into chaos.

But this moment was a gift. And she was smart enough, perceptive enough to recognize it for what it was. She felt the shift like tectonic plates beneath her feet, a sharpness in the air, a lightness in her chest.

In that still, small moment, the dying world seemed so far away.

These woods were a separate place full of wonder and enchantment, tangled dreams and wild wishes and stars close enough to touch.

It was magic.

15

R aven awoke to the sound of voices.

It seemed an impossible feat to fall asleep inches from two hundred pounds of lethal predator, but she had.

She went rigid as the loud male voices pierced her consciousness. Instantly, she was wide awake, her heart thumping, ice streaking her veins. Her eyes sprang open. She searched the small clearing, scanning the empty ground on either side of her, the trees towering all around her.

Shadow and Luna had smelled the bikers long before Raven heard them. The wolves had already vanished into their den or hidden somewhere in the cluster of pine, elm, and maple trees and heavy underbrush.

Twenty yards and a copse of trees were all that separated the den from the public viewing area along the flagstone path. Wolves were private creatures, her father had always insisted. He'd refused to cut down the trees, even when guests complained.

Now, Raven was grateful for the cover. She sat up slowly, her back aching, a crick in her neck. She ran her tongue over her furry teeth. Her mouth tasted sour. What she wouldn't give for a toothbrush. Her scalp itched, and she felt unwashed.

She strained to hear the voices over the rumbling of her stomach. She couldn't catch more than a stray word; she needed to get closer. There were two choices. She could remain hidden—and relatively safe—here, or she could creep closer and try to overhear something useful.

She'd hoped the bikers would be gone by now. They weren't.

Knowledge is power. One of her father's favorite phrases. He'd taught her how to take everything in first—details of her surroundings, potential predators, allies, and prey—then act only after analyzing the available information. The more she knew about these thugs, the better.

She crawled on her belly beneath several pine boughs, the scent of sap and dead, crumbling leaves strong in her nostrils. She was careful to brush away sticks and twigs, to make as little noise as possible. Pausing just behind a wide branch, she ensured she was hidden in deep shadows while still offered a clear view.

It was just past dawn. The air was chilly—her breath puffed in white swirls. The sky was like glass, so sharp and clear she could almost believe she could see clear through to heaven, or maybe the future.

Four men leaned against the guardrail, three of them smoking as they gazed into the hybrid enclosure. They all wore guns holstered to their hips, rifles strapped across their brawny shoulders and chests. There was Cerberus, the leader; Ryker, the killer; Jagger, the gaunt, pony-tailed one; and Damien, the young redhead who'd nearly shot Phil.

"You sure you saw it?" asked Cerberus.

"Plain as day," Damien said. "It was white as a ghost and huge. The biggest wolf I've ever seen, even for a mod."

Cerberus's grin widened. He patted Damien approvingly on the back. "Good boy."

Damien smiled eagerly, his pale, freckled skin almost blushing.

So it was Damien who'd surprised her at the bear padlock last night. She shivered involuntarily. She couldn't quite figure him out. He hadn't shot the pharmacist, but he'd been about to. He was so much younger than the others, barely older than she was. She knew logically that age had nothing to do with it. He might be worse than Ryker.

He was disconcertingly handsome, but there was a hardness in the slash of his cheekbones, the narrow jut of his chin. He was obviously eager to prove himself, and that was dangerous.

"How do we make it show itself, then?" Ryker asked in a bored tone. "I'm starving. Bones is making breakfast. He found actual pancake mix."

Jagger stood next to Ryker and blew out a ring of cigarette smoke. "Did you see how much food is here? This place is a gold mine."

"And mine it we shall," Cerberus said. "In due time."

Ryker looked like he wanted to roll his eyes in disgust. But he didn't—he knew who was boss.

"We must be patient, my friends." Cerberus had a sophisticated air about him, a civilized facade, like he might strangle you with one hand while sipping expensive wine from a crystal glass with the other. Scorpio, Jagger, and Ryker were his guard dogs, brutes who killed on command. Or in Ryker's case, just for the hell of it.

Ryker rubbed his goatee, his eyebrows dark slashes over eyes black as silt. He was a killer, maybe the most dangerous of all of them. Raven had seen the look on his face when he'd shot Carl. He didn't kill in self-defense or because he'd been told to; he killed because he enjoyed it.

A leaf fluttered to Raven's left. She flinched and craned her neck.

The black wolf crouched not five feet from her, staring intently at the men beyond the fence, his ears flat and lips pulling back. She hadn't heard him approach. Likely, Luna was nearby as well.

Stay back, she whispered to them in her mind. *Stay hidden.*

Ryker bent and picked up a loose, fist-sized rock from the path. Over the years, much of the flagstone had cracked. Her father had never gotten around to getting it fixed. Ryker hurled the rock into the enclosure. It struck the trunk of a slim sugar maple with a resounding crack.

Cerberus laughed. A half-second later, Damien laughed, too, his gaze flicking eagerly to the man's face.

"That's one way to do it." Jagger's voice was deep and rasping, like he'd been smoking for fifty years—though he couldn't have been older than thirty.

Jagger picked up his own rock and threw it at the pine tree Raven was crouched behind. The branches shook, pine needles raining down on her head.

Shadow growled.

Raven wanted to shush him, but she couldn't afford to make a sound. He was used to being the predator; it wasn't in his nature to act the prey, to live in fear. She stared at the wolf as hard as she could, desperate to somehow communicate her thoughts. *Be quiet. Be still. Don't let them see you.*

"I heard one," Jagger drawled. "Draw 'em out."

He and Ryker hurled several more rocks. With each crack, Shadow's growl grew louder, more fierce.

She wanted to reach out and touch him, try to calm him, but

didn't dare. He was no dog. He was still a wild animal, incredibly powerful and driven by primal instincts she couldn't begin to understand.

A rock struck the trunk of an elm a foot from Shadow's head.

With a snarl, Shadow sprang from the protection of the trees.

Shadow halted thirty feet from the fence, tail stiff behind him. He growled deep in his throat, the ruff on his neck bristling, making him look even larger and more menacing. His lips stretched back until he was showing every one of his forty-two sharp, gleaming teeth.

Damien whistled.

"Look at the pelt on that one, boys!" Cerberus crowed. "It's gorgeous!"

Jagger lifted his rifle and aimed at the wolf.

Raven tensed, longing to leap out after Shadow, to defend him, to *do* something, but she couldn't. If she revealed herself now, they would take her and do terrible things.

She needed to stay hidden. There was nothing she could do but watch in growing dismay, praying these maggots didn't harm the wolves.

"Easy now." Cerberus put his hand on the barrel of Jagger's rifle and forced him to lower it. "Not yet. We don't want to waste the meat or ruin the pelt."

"Whatever you say, boss," Jagger said with an easy shrug. He fixed his gaze on Shadow. His onyx eyes glittered. "I call that one."

Ryker seized another rock and heaved it at the wolf. It struck Shadow in the flank.

Shadow leapt forward with a savage snarl. Behind him, Luna plunged out of the trees. She halted beside him, snapping her jaws, ears flattened against her skull, eyes blazing.

Cerberus straightened with a gasp. His entire face lit with a greedy, rapacious desire. "Well, looky there. Here he is, in all his glory. You were right, kid. He's fit for a king."

Dread coiled in Raven's stomach. She hated the way the men were looking at the wolves—as if they were trophies. She dug her nails into her palms to keep from screaming.

Cerberus turned away from the fence. "The white wolf is mine. No one touches him until tomorrow."

"How long we staying here?" Ryker asked.

"Antsy already, are you?" Cerberus dropped the stub of his cigarette and ground it out with the heel of his boot. "Everything in its time."

Ryker stepped in close to Cerberus. "We're wasting time. There's too much to do. We can't afford to waste days here and squander—"

Cerberus's expression went hard. "When I want your opinion, I'll ask for it."

Ryker scowled. For half an instant, he looked mutinous. Then his face cleared, and he smiled lazily. "Sure thing, boss."

Cerberus turned his back on Ryker. "Let's go."

Ryker stayed behind as the others followed Cerberus along the path back toward the lodge. Damien glanced back at Ryker, a shadow darkening his face. Then he turned and left with the others.

Ryker chucked two more stones at the wolves—one striking Luna on her right foreleg, the other hitting Shadow's muzzle.

The wolves fell back, growling and snapping in impotent fury.

Ryker only laughed darkly. His expression was scornful, malignant. He made the shape of a gun with his fingers and pointed it first at Shadow, then Luna. "Bang, bang. You're dead."

16

For a long time after Ryker left, Raven didn't move from beneath the pine tree. Anger sizzled through her like an electrical current—but also fear, knotted and jagged. And not just for herself.

Shaking, she gritted her teeth. How dare they mock the wolves? How dare they hurt such wild, beautiful creatures? She wanted to hit something, to pound her fists against the nearest tree and scream out her frustration. Or better yet, take out her anger on the bikers. Maybe claw Ryker's face a bit, give him a taste of his own medicine. The thought gave her a grim satisfaction.

Finally, she forced herself to sit up and brushed needles, dirt, and dead leaves from her hair and clothes. Lying here wouldn't fix anything. It wasn't going to get her any further away from these thugs. She needed to move.

The wolves had retreated to the safety of their den. Cautiously, she stood and followed them, slow and tentative.

When Raven stepped into the clearing, Luna whirled on her, lips curling back from her fangs.

Raven dropped immediately to a submissive sitting position.

But that wasn't enough for Luna. She growled and lunged at Raven. The wolf reared up and struck both great paws against Raven's shoulders. Raven was slammed to the ground.

The back of her head smacked the ground hard. Pain jarred her spine. Raven sucked in air that wouldn't come, the force of the blow knocking the breath out of her. She stared up at Luna, shocked and petrified.

Paws still on her shoulders, pressing her down, Luna lowered her huge head inches from Raven's face and snarled. Hot breath spewed against Raven's cheeks. Saliva splattered on her chin, her lips.

Teeth bared, Luna snapped her jaws again and again in Raven's face. Gaping jaws, a raw red throat, and gleaming, needle-sharp fangs filled Raven's vision. Her heart shuddered inside her chest. She flinched, certain the she-wolf was about to tear her face off.

Humans had just hurled rocks at Luna. Of course, she'd be enraged. Of course, she'd want to take revenge on the nearest human. It made sense. If Raven were a wolf, she would feel the same way.

She had her whittling knife in her pocket. But just like with Shadow, it could do little damage, while Luna's jaws could crush bones, shred ligaments, tendons, and muscles, pulverizing whatever flesh she sank her teeth into—all within a second or two. Fighting back would only enrage the wolf further.

Raven forced herself to remain limp, hoping Luna was only posturing, hoping she didn't decide Raven was a threat better off dead.

Shadow growled. Luna snapped her head up.

Raven took the second of diversion to shield her face with her hands. She tried to curl her lower half into a ball, protecting her vulnerable stomach, but Luna was still standing on Raven's shoulders, pinning her to the ground.

Abruptly, Luna was shoved aside. Shadow shouldered into her, pushing her off Raven. He nipped at Luna's flank as she spun, a growl already rumbling deep in her throat.

Luna came back snarling and snapping, this time at Shadow. The black wolf stood his ground between Raven and Luna. Raven scrambled a few feet back on her elbows, gasping for breath, her pulse a roar in her ears.

The wolves stared at each other, standing stiffly, ears back, growling. For whatever reason, Shadow wanted to take a chance on Raven; Luna clearly did not. Luna didn't trust Raven, didn't like her, considered her an outsider, an interloper. Which she was.

Humans had trapped Luna, beat her with whips, and forced her to battle to the death in the fighting ring. Humans had jeered at her, thrown rocks, caged her. Humans had hunted her kind since the dawn of time.

It was a miracle that Luna hadn't already crushed Raven's windpipe with a single bite.

Luna growled in warning, her head lowered. Shadow growled right back. Neither gave way. Neither submitted.

Raven remembered what her father had taught her about pack behavior when one wolf challenged another. For a lesser-ranked wolf, a battle of domination and submission would ensue, sometimes to the death or the exclusion of the losing wolf from the pack.

But not with these two. They were alphas, partners, equals.

Then Shadow gave a low whine in the back of his throat. He loped to Luna, pressed in and nuzzled his mate's side. She nipped at him angrily, but didn't bite or shy away.

He licked her muzzle. She snorted.

He licked her again, whining, his tail lifting hopefully.

This time, she didn't nip at him. Conceding, she lowered her head and tucked it beneath his, rubbing her muzzle against his shoulders and neck.

The fight was over. For now.

Luna settled herself on the other side of the clearing, as far away from Raven as she could get. Shadow sank down beside Luna and buried his muzzle in the soft fur of her neck. She, in turn, rested her head on his back and fixed her unblinking amber eyes on Raven.

I'm watching you, her gaze said.

Dread seeded itself in Raven's stomach as she watched them, a dark, ugly fear sprouting black roots. Cerberus and Ryker wanted these wolves for something. To kill for sport? Something equally horrible?

The bikers would be back. And next time, they wouldn't just stand outside the fence.

She'd hoped the bikers would hunker down for the night and take off in the morning to wherever they were headed. She'd been naive. And very, very wrong.

She wrapped her arms around herself, unable to stop shivering. Hunger gnawed at her empty stomach. Her mouth was so dry it felt caked in sand. She coughed.

Raven froze. A single cough didn't mean anything, not really. People coughed all the time. She was just clearing her throat. That's all. Nothing more. *Please, please be nothing more.*

She closed her eyes for a moment, mentally counting the days. Four since exposure. The cold symptoms should have started yesterday or today. If she was infected, she would know soon.

Raven opened her eyes. She couldn't stay here. She had to run.

She was probably at least a two-days' hike on foot from the nearest town after Clay Creek. But with the Hydra virus infecting everything it touched, towns were far more dangerous than the woods now.

There was still the cabin, but it was fifty miles away. The cabin, with its rough-hewn walls and the raggedy smoke-blue curtains she'd picked out and sewn herself when she was twelve. The floor was worn and scuffed from years of use, the windows filmed and scuzzy, the cabinet doors nearly falling off their hinges, a rack of ancient copper pots hanging from the low ceiling. The porcelain farmer's sink in the corner with the blue-and-green gingham curtain she and her mother had picked out together, on one of her mother's rare good days.

All those times she'd hunted with her father, returning so tired, she'd fallen onto the dumpy mattress fully clothed, without removing her boots; her father curling up on the floor—no blanket, not even a pillow.

The cabin was as much hers as anyone's. It was a safe place. The place she'd felt closest to her father. It even held a few pleasant memories of her mother.

The cabin was where she needed to go.

Her backpack was still in the lodge. She couldn't survive more than a day or two in the woods without it. She needed her snares for catching small game. There were none stored at the cabin.

More importantly, she needed her water filtration packets and Lifestraw so she could drink from the river. She needed her flint to make fire, she needed her compass, her tent for warmth and shelter.

She wouldn't survive for long without her backpack.

It didn't take her long to decide. Tonight, under cover of darkness, she would go back and get it.

The front entrance was too dangerous with all the thugs congregating around the lodge and the Grizzly Grill. She would escape out the back gate.

In the distance, the bonobos screeched grumpily. The bears growled at each other with low moans. They were all hungry.

She forced herself to tear her gaze from Luna's piercing, judgmental eyes.

There was nothing she could do about that.

She had to think of her own survival now.

17

As morning gave way to afternoon and afternoon to evening, a warm front descended from the north. The sun set achingly slow, until finally the sky darkened to night. The air filled with the trill of crickets and cicadas. Stars spattered the glossy black of the sky.

Raven set off for the lodge as fog drifted over the treeline like ribbons of tulle.

After checking to make sure the coast was clear, she locked each gate of the double fence. Shadow and Luna watched her go, still and silent.

She pulled out her whittling knife, unfolded it, and gripped it in one hand as she crept along the enclosures. She passed the porcupine pen. Duke and Duchess bustled out of their little house, quills bristling. They hissed at her in outrage for daring to interrupt their nocturnal habits—whatever those might be.

Hera ruffled her feathers from the aptly named eagle's nest, a two-story wire-mesh enclosure with a tree to rest on and lovely views of the park. She sat serenely on her perch, talons gripping the wooden pole, her beady raptor eyes tracking Raven's every movement.

The otters chirped as she inched past their glass-front habitat. She could barely make out the shape of one of them—either Whiskers or Mo—lounging on his rock, his eyes glittering as he watched her.

She hesitated at the cinderblock maintenance shed. The tranq guns and the emergency rifles were stored inside. She couldn't justify leaving them again. The bikers were dangerous. She needed to protect herself.

Quietly, she unlocked and opened the rusted metal door. The corrugated roof leaked. Junk cluttered every corner—coils of rusting wire, broken power tools, buckets of old batteries, shelves of solar lamps, hammers, and wrenches.

Everything was coated in a filmy layer of grease and grime. Dust swirled in the blurry moonlight filtering through the filthy window. Her mask protected her from the worst of it, though a tickling sensation irritated her throat.

She swallowed a cough, forcing it down. She hesitated for a moment—but she didn't feel the urge to cough again. *Only dust*, she told herself. *It was only dust.*

She maneuvered around the huge metal workbench that looked like it hadn't been used in thirty years, sidestepping two large containers of gasoline shoved against the wall below the gun rack.

She shoved two tranq guns into her waistband, stuffed her cargo pockets with ammo and extra darts encased in metal cylinders, and hooked the strap of the hunting rifle over her shoulder. She wiped her hands on her pants as she left the shed and quietly closed the door behind her.

Three minutes later, she reached the lodge.

Voices boomed from inside, raucous laughter and boisterous

shouts. It sounded like they'd found the Grizzly Grill's alcohol supply. The front windows glowed with the light of several solar lamps.

Relief flared through her. Her window, at least, was dark.

A cinderblock was propped up on its side beneath her window. She'd used it to sneak in and out before. Not that she had anywhere illicit or exciting to go. When she was younger, she would stretch out on her back on Vlad's tiger house and count all the stars, wondering if maybe her mother was staring up at the exact same sky, thinking about Raven. On her seventeenth birthday, Raven had come to the conclusion that she wasn't, and never had.

Raven straightened the cinderblock, used it as a stool, and peeked inside her window. Everything was dark, drenched in shadows. The door was closed. She grasped the windowsill and carefully inched it up. The lock had broken years ago. There had never been a reason to fix it.

The window scraped against the wood. Raven paused, stiffening.

No change. The loud voices continued. Nothing moved inside. Nothing moved outside.

She pushed the window all the way up, braced her elbows on the frame, and used the cinderblock to push herself up. She clambered inside, careful not to kick or bump anything on her dresser directly to the left of the window.

She stood in her bedroom, letting her eyes adjust to the darkness. Rumpled bed. Clothes strewn across the floor. Dresser cluttered with dusty wooden figurines and scattered wood shavings. It smelled like something unwashed, mixed with a whiff of her green apple shampoo.

Exactly how she'd left it.

She found the faded army-green hiking backpack leaning

against her bed and yanked a camouflaged raincoat from her closet. With her undershirt, a sweater, and her raincoat—waterproof, but with an inner synthetic lining for warmth—she should have enough layers to withstand the cold October nights out-of-doors. She wore her good hiking boots and two pairs of socks to prevent blisters.

She pulled two granola bars from a side pocket, unwrapped them with fingers trembling from hunger, and practically inhaled them. She took a long swig from her water bottle and wiped her mouth with the back of her hand, already feeling better.

She paused, scanning the shadowed room for anything else she might need. Something glinted in the back of her closet. The old hoverboard her mother had bought for her birthday, that Raven had refused to use on principle.

Maybe it would come in useful. She could travel faster, without leaving tracks. She grabbed the hoverboard, too. It was solar-powered and fully charged.

She unzipped her pack, shoved the board halfway in, and dragged it over to the window. She had no way to lower the pack silently. She'd just have to dump it and hope no one heard. She hefted it and pushed it out the window. It hit the ground with a thud.

Still, the voices down the hall were loud enough to cover her movements. They were so loud she could almost make out the words. She turned away from the window, straining her ears. If she opened the door a crack, she might be able to hear them...

She glanced at the window and the door, torn.

Maybe they were talking about the wolves. Maybe they were talking about her. The more she knew, the better prepared she'd be.

Raven crept toward her bedroom door. She grasped the handle, twisted, and slowly pulled the door open about six inches.

The long hallway was dark. The doors to the two guest

bedrooms on this side were open, but no light filtered out. There were three more guest bedrooms on the other side of the kitchen.

Her father's door was closed. She let out a relieved breath. The bikers probably smelled the stench of sickness still emanating from the bed. She'd thrown out the sheets, pillowcases, and comforter, but it didn't seem to matter. The bedroom still smelled like death and despair.

At the end of the hallway spilled a semi-circle of warm yellow light from the lanterns in the kitchen. Thick swirls of smoke hung heavily in the air. In the center of the kitchen, she could see at least a half-dozen men hunched around the scarred wooden table she'd eaten breakfast at almost every day of her life.

They were playing some sort of card game, drinking and smoking, placing bets and roaring with laughter, scowling with frustration, a few bleary and unfocused, all of them drunk.

She could make out a thread of conversation over the ruckus— closer than the kitchen table. A man's shoulder jutted against the opposite wall into the space at the end of the hallway—leather vest, long, greasy ponytail. Jagger. The others were likely sitting at the bar chairs at the counter peninsula, just around the corner from her line of sight.

"When are the others coming?" She recognized Jagger's low, gravelly voice.

"Phillips went to get them." Cerberus's deep, ringing baritone was unmistakable. "He left yesterday afternoon. By the time they gather their supplies, get the truck, and make it back...I'd reckon sometime tomorrow night."

"I'd kill for a working SmartFlex." Damien's voice. "This lack of communication blows."

"Wouldn't we all, kid," Cerberus said with a dark chuckle. "But look on the bright side. Instead of focusing on what's been destroyed, focus on what we can build from the rubble. A new world. A new society, with order and rules that make sense—even better than the last one."

"How many men is he bringing?" Jagger asked.

"I told him twenty. We'll need that many to load all that food."

"There aren't enough beds for them," Damien said.

"They can sleep on the floor, or out in the tiger's cage for all I care." Ryker's voice—smooth as honey to hide the poison beneath.

"We'll make do," Cerberus said. "We always do. This was a lucky break. We need to share the wealth."

"And then we head back home?" Ryker asked.

"Thought you wanted that girl," Jagger said.

The hairs on Raven's neck stood on end at the mention of herself. Her stomach lurched. She gripped the door with whitened knuckles.

"To hell with her," Ryker spat. "This place is creepy. Don't you feel it? All those savage beasts screaming and howling all night long?"

Cerberus let out a booming laugh. "Homesick? Don't you worry. After we load up our goodies, you can burn this place to the ground for all I care."

"And the wolves? Do we get to pick?" Jagger asked.

"Let me guess," Cerberus said, mirth in his voice. "Damien wants the tiger."

Ryker snorted. "You'll have to grow into that one, boy. You still have to earn your chops." His tone was teasing, but there was something mocking in the way he spoke.

"I will." Damien sounded frustrated, petulant. "Don't worry about me."

"Enough sitting around," Cerberus said. "The night is young! We've got work to do." A chair pushed back, scraping against the tile. Cerberus's broad back appeared as he shoved the chair in place, tattoos squirming across his neck and bulging arms. "Remember, the white one is mine."

Heart hammering in her throat, Raven shut the door and stumbled back. More of them were coming. They were going to take all the food in the storage buildings—the food she was depending on to stay alive.

Her stomach twisted. What were they going to do to the animals? Kill them for sport? For meat? Burn them alive in their pens?

She had to get out of there, think things through somewhere else, somewhere safe. She lurched for the window.

The bedroom door swung open.

18

Raven had just enough time to dive into the shadows between her dresser and the bed, hunkering down beneath the window. It was a pathetic hiding spot. But with no light, she might have the barest chance. As long as she didn't give herself away, didn't move or breathe.

Carefully, silently, she reached into her pocket for the knife. She had to shift her thighs for access, leaning hard on the side of the dresser. She pulled it out, but didn't flick it open. It would make noise. She grasped the handle with both hands and held it to her chest, knuckles white, every muscle taut.

The intruder was nothing but a murky shape among murkier shadows. He shut the door behind him. She heard the click of the lock being turned. There was a soft thumping sound. Then, silence.

Her lungs burned for oxygen. Her body screamed at her to suck in deep, ragged breaths. But she couldn't. She breathed shallowly through her nose, fighting against the panic slithering up her throat, squeezing her windpipe.

The intruder was still completely silent, except for his breathing. Laughter from the kitchen filtered through the door, dim and far away.

What was he doing? Had he spotted her? Did he know she was there? Was it a trap? The not-knowing wound tighter and tighter inside her, until she was about to crack wide open.

Her eyes had adjusted to the dark. His had not. She gathered her courage and leaned forward cautiously, peering past the edge of the dresser.

She recognized the tall, lanky figure. Damien slumped against the door, head back, his breathing uneven and rasping. His arms hung at his sides, his hands clenched into fists. His expression was grim, tense. It looked like his eyes were closed. It was hard to tell.

Outside, the fog thinned for a moment. Moonlight poured through the window, bathing everything in a silvery glow.

Maybe she should have ducked back behind the dresser. She didn't.

Damien was just standing there. His chest rose and fell rapidly. There was something uneasy and haggard in his face. His piercings glinted. As he breathed, his fists slowly unclenched, his tense expression relaxing, like he was free now, like he'd just escaped something.

She tightened her grip on the knife handle. Her palms were damp. Her pulse thudded in her throat. She'd never attacked anyone before, animal or human. She didn't want to start now. *Just go, just go.*

Instead, Damien opened his eyes and looked straight at her.

For an infinite second, she stared back at him, frozen.

He looked at her blankly, as if she were a ghost he didn't quite believe was real. Until his gaze lowered and fixed on the knife in her hands.

Raven exploded into motion. She leapt to her feet and lunged at him, flicking the blade open as she ran, no thought in her head but to stop him from shouting and warning the eight hardened criminals sitting less than twenty feet away.

She thrust the knife to his throat before his face had even registered surprise.

He grunted and let out a curse. "What—"

"Shut up!" she hissed. "Do or say anything to alert your friends, and I swear to you, I'll slit your throat."

He raised both hands in a gesture of surrender. "And if you do that, they'll come looking for me, find me dead, and then they'll know you're here."

"I thought they already did."

He gave the faintest shake of his head, wincing as she pressed the blade deeper. "Suspecting is different than knowing. Ryker saw which way you turned. He wanted you. So we followed, driving around aimlessly, looking for you until we stumbled on this place. They think you're here somewhere, but they don't know. They've all been distracted by the food and the zoo. You kill one of their own, what do you think is going to happen? They'll hunt you down in earnest."

"You're insane if you think I'm just gonna let you go."

The hard planes of his face were shadowed in moonlight. He attempted a smile, but it came out more like a grimace. "You can. I won't say anything. I told them I was going for a piss. But really, I just needed—Look, I'll just go back and drink and eat and laugh, and none of them'll be the wiser. You don't know us, but we're not bad people. I'm not a bad person. We look tough, but—"

She shot him a scathing look. "Nice try. I know what you did. I saw what happened to Carl. I saw you point your gun in Phil's face."

His eyes widened. "You were at the pharmacy."

"That's right. Your pretty face and your pretty lies won't work. I know what you are."

"You don't know what things are like out there, how bad it's gotten."

"I saw Clay Creek, what was happening there."

He started to shake his head, stiffening as the blade sliced through a layer of his skin. "That's nothing. The world is chaos. It's kill or be killed, eat or be eaten."

"Carl was unarmed."

"Okay." His eyes flickered around the room, searching for something, probably a weapon, but coming up empty. He pursed his lips, trying a different tack. "Okay. Ryker is...I know what it looks like. It's been six weeks since this Hydra bioweapon started killing everyone. The national supply chain broke down over three weeks ago. Do you know how much surplus food stores hold? Three days. People are murdering each other for a can of green beans. If you don't align yourself with the type of people who can protect you, then you're already dead."

"And who *are* the people you're with?"

"They're a gang, call themselves the Headhunters. They've been around for years, operating in Georgia and parts of North Carolina. But once the virus started destroying everything, they saw a window, an opportunity. They're traders and service providers. Surviving communities exchange their resources in fair trade for services rendered, like protection from thieves, marauders, and various unsavory criminals.

"The Headhunters travel around scavenging, searching for anything of value. They can get people whatever they want or need —illegal weapons, drugs, expensive, rare medications. Pretty much anything."

She caught how he spoke of the Headhunters as "they" and not "we," trying to distance himself and generate sympathy. She scowled. "What other kinds of services?" She could guess, but she needed to know. "Why do you want me?"

"I'm not sure. I'm just a low-level guy. I don't know everything—"

She tilted the curved razor-edge of the blade just enough to draw blood. "Tell me."

He swallowed. The edge of the knife bobbed along with his Adam's apple. "Sometimes, they trade in...people."

Her blood went cold.

"There's no law anymore. No one to stop those with certain... appetites. They pay for people. Mostly girls. Young, pretty ones that can be trained." His lips pressed together. "I'm not a part of any of that. Mostly it's trading in good things, helping people survive, get what they need. I've—I've never even killed anyone." He said it like a confession, like it shamed him.

Me either, she almost said. But that would've defeated the purpose of the knife—and the threat behind it. Just because she hadn't killed before didn't mean she wouldn't. If she had to.

"Let me go," Damien said.

"No way."

He sighed. "Then we're at a standstill. Either you kill me, or you don't. Eventually, Ryker is going to come looking for me, and then what are you going to do?"

She had no idea, but she wasn't going to tell him that. "Then I'll kill you now and take whatever head start I can get."

"I won't say anything." His voice was still even. He didn't sound afraid. "Isn't that worth the risk? You kill me, they hunt you down, whether you have ten seconds or ten minutes, they will find you. You let me go, there's a chance I'm true to my word, and they'll never know you were here."

She despised his logic, but it rang true. An image of Shadow's jaws closing around her throat flashed through her mind. *An alpha was the one with the power to kill, but chose not to.* She didn't want to kill this guy. Even though she was fairly certain he was lying through his pretty teeth. She didn't want blood on her hands.

He looked down at her, his expression unreadable. "Are you going to let me go now?"

Abruptly she was aware of how close she was to him, his breath rustling her hair, the hardness of his body, spare and wiry, pressed against her own. His piercings glinted in the moonlight. She could make out the individual lashes brushing his cheeks when he blinked.

Her breath caught in her throat. "No."

"Yes," he said, "you are. Because you know I'm right."

"You're the bad guy."

"That's a matter of perspective."

"Tell that to Carl."

"You're running out of time," he said, his voice still infuriatingly calm. But his frequent swallows betrayed his nervousness.

She watched the blade ride up and down his throat. She hated that he was right. She hated that she didn't trust this guy as far as she could throw him. But in the end, she had little choice. Only one option made sense.

"Fine," she said grudgingly. She inhaled sharply and stepped back, removing the knife from his neck but keeping it up and ready, half-expecting him to scream. Or attack her.

He did neither. He stood still, hands loose at his sides. The way he was looking at her, curious, a little wary, fascinated even—it was jarring. She didn't like it. She wasn't one of the animals to be stared at, examined with impunity.

"What is your name?" he asked, that cunning, fox-eyed look back on his face.

"None of your business."

A ghost of a smile flickered across his face.

She pointed her knife at him. "Stay back."

From the kitchen, someone shouted. "Damien! Hurry the hell up! Let's go!"

Both Raven and the boy froze. Would he yell now? Betray his promise and reveal her presence? How many seconds did she have? Five, ten? Not enough.

"Run," he said. "Run, and don't look back."

She ran.

Raven pivoted, feeling far too exposed and vulnerable, and clambered out the window. Her heart raced, waiting for a knife or a bullet to the back. None came.

She dropped to the ground, hoisted her pack over her shoulders, and ran without a backward glance.

The fog was thicker now, drifting in hazy white ribbons, making visibility poor. Behind her, a few lights bobbed like spotlights in the murky gloom.

She swerved sharply and plunged behind the meat storage building. She pressed her back against the concrete and peered around the corner. The fog both helped and hindered her. What hid Raven also hid any skulking Headhunters. She could barely see forty feet ahead or behind her.

She watched the bobbing flashlights draw nearer. She held her breath, waiting for the cries of alarm. They didn't come. There was no shouting. No Headhunters running toward her, guns blazing.

Maybe that boy had kept his word after all. She couldn't understand it, but now wasn't the time to figure it out.

She eased around the far corner of the building, heart thudding, as she waited for the group of Headhunters to pass. She waited for their voices to dim, for their footfalls to fade into silence.

In her frazzled state, she didn't remember the hoverboard until she'd started running again. She was too scared to stop. She stayed off the main path and kept to the rear of the exhibits, weeds and thorns snagging at her pant legs. She ran and ran, legs pumping, adrenaline shooting through her veins, cold breath searing her throat.

She made it past the reptile house, the bonobos, the otters, porcupines, and eagle, the ostriches. And then she was circling back onto the flagstone path, rounding the enclosure with Kodiak and Sage still sleeping soundly. She was almost at the rear gate, about to turn into the narrow space between the bear and hybrid paddocks.

Sudden voices to her right. Flashlights wavering wildly. Echoing laughter. Several Headhunters were clustered by the timber wolf enclosure.

She couldn't see clearly in the mist, couldn't make out what they were doing—

She skidded to a halt, panic roaring through her as the first gunshot cracked the air.

19

Echo let out the first cry, a cross between a pained whimper and an agonized howl. She heard the terrible thump of his body hitting the ground. The men laughed and high-fived each other, hooting and yelling in celebration.

Their backs were turned to her. They didn't see her take several shaking steps toward them. Didn't see her standing numb and horrified on the path, fog swirling around her, exposed for anyone to see but too stunned to move.

Five men leaned over the timber wolves' paddock, rifles tucked against their shoulders as they fired into the enclosure.

She recognized Cerberus, Jagger, Ryker, Scorpio. The fifth Headhunter was half-turned in the other direction. When he swung back toward the enclosure, a flashlight beam caught his face—angled cheekbones, narrow chin, spiky fox-red hair, the gleam of metal piercings.

A sharp bitterness welled in the back of her throat. Damien may not have ratted her out, but he was one of them all the same. A

Headhunter. A thug and a killer. Cruel and malicious, no different than the rest of these repugnant thugs.

Another gunshot drew her attention.

The Headhunters were shooting the wolves. For sport. For fun.

The timber wolves had fled into the protection of the trees, desperately trying to evade the thunderous noises and explosions of pain. Aspen and Titus were snarling and growling fiercely. Loki and Suki were whimpering. Shika let out a long, mournful howl of despair.

The Headhunters moved around the fence, hurling insults and laughing. When they couldn't spot the wolves, they shot randomly into the underbrush

Titus burst out of the trees, charging at the Headhunters in a desperate bid to protect his pack. Ryker aimed and fired.

Titus took two staggering steps and fell with a moan. He didn't get up.

Cerberus and Ryker laughed. Jagger slapped Ryker on the back. Damien's expression was indifferent, his eyes hard and blank.

Run! Raven's brain screamed at her. *RUN!* But she couldn't. Her legs were lead. She felt dizzy, disconnected, her brain stuffed with cotton.

Instead of fleeing for the safety of the woods, she backed away, spun, and stumbled on wobbly legs to the gate she'd left less than an hour before. She opened the outer gate, slipped inside, locked it. Crossed the no man's land barrier, and repeated the same motions on autopilot, hardly realizing what she was doing.

Mist curled around her legs. Everything had taken on an eerie, silvery glow. The fog was creeping ever closer, almost like it was alive. Like it would take everything she cared about and devour it, one murky, malignant mouthful at a time.

More gunshots split the air. She flinched.

Another wolf screamed in agony. She wasn't sure which one. Suki or Shika? Her mind churned with revulsion and helpless fury.

She had to keep moving. She staggered inside the hybrid enclosure, still not sure what she was doing, not even certain this was the safer option. The hybrids might be so worked up and frantic at the gunshots, they could tear her to pieces where she stood.

But they didn't.

When she entered the clearing near the den, Shadow's great head appeared. He whimpered, his beautiful amber eyes brimming with apprehension and bewilderment.

She went down on her hands and knees and crawled to the edge of the den. She shrugged off her pack and collapsed on the cold, damp ground, shivering uncontrollably.

All this time, she'd been hiding and plotting her own escape instead of *doing* something. She understood now what they meant to do with the wolves, with all the animals. One by one, the Headhunters were going to slaughter them, butcher them for their own sick entertainment.

A wretched, furious helplessness overwhelmed her. Shame and regret burned bitter in the back of her throat. If she'd acted last night, or even hours earlier, Echo wouldn't be dead. Titus wouldn't be dead.

You were going to do the same thing, a voice whispered in her mind. But it wasn't the same thing. Hers was an act of mercy, tranquilizing the animals first so they'd never feel the sting of the bullet, so they'd pass in peace, not with violence, terror, and suffering.

The way her father had spared Zachariah. The way he'd wanted her to spare him.

Shadow stood over her. He nosed her trembling shoulder with his muzzle. He licked her cheek. Luna appeared at his side.

The white wolf stepped over Raven like she wasn't there and

paused in the center of the small clearing. She growled, her lips peeled back from her fangs, her ears flattened against her skull. Instinctively, she understood something terrible was happening, and she was angry. Luna wanted to fight.

Raven sat up. She wiped dirt from her cheek and brushed off the pine needles. Her bones vibrated beneath her skin. She tasted her heart in her mouth. A chill crept over her, filling her veins with a cold, crystallized anger.

She was done hiding. She was done letting fear rule her.

She couldn't run. She refused to run.

She couldn't leave the animals behind to be slaughtered. Animals she'd known since childhood. Vlad, Kodiak and Sage, Suki and Aspen, Electra, Mo, and Gizmo and all the others. Animals she'd spent so much time resenting she'd forgotten she also loved them.

She was all alone. It was just her in the whole wide broken world.

She was the only one who could do something. The only one who could try to stop this.

Haven was *her* home. *Her* refuge. It was her job to protect it, to defend it.

But there were nine Headhunters to her one. And tomorrow night, twenty more would arrive.

There was only one option, one chance to save what she could. They might die anyway—half-tamed, zoo-raised captives unable to fend for themselves in the wild.

It was dangerous. Maybe reckless. Certainly stupid.

She would free the animals.

All of them. Every last one.

20

It was after midnight when the Headhunters' cacophony died down to silence. Raven waited another hour, crouched at the foot of the den, every muscle tensed, anger zapping through her like a live wire.

Fog drifted, snaking between the trees. Luna was sleeping in the den. Shadow was stretched out a few feet from Raven. He was awake, alert, though his head was resting on his paws, his ears flicking this way and that as he listened to the animals express their anxiety and confusion.

The bonobos screeched and hooted, pleading and begging for food. Kodiak bellowed hungrily. The remaining timber wolves howled in grief, their keening wail rising, rising toward the sliver of the moon and the hard, uncaring stars.

Raven could make out three distinct voices. Three still alive; that meant three dead.

She clenched one of the tranquilizer guns in one hand. The hunting rifle was slung over her shoulder—fully loaded.

She would do her best to make sure the rest of Haven's creatures lived through the night. After that, she didn't know.

With the world outside dead and dying, maybe there would be enough food for the animals. Without the humans encroaching on their habitats or hunting them to extinction, maybe they could survive out there, finally live in freedom. Perhaps one positive thing could come from all this.

There were probably better plans. Smarter ideas. But she was out of time. And she was alone.

Her dad would have known what to do. Whatever his flaws, he would've stood beside her and defended their home. And he would've done a far better job than she could on her own. The sudden ache in her chest stole her breath; it was so painful.

Only a few days ago, she couldn't wait to get away from her father. Now she missed him with a desperateness she couldn't have put into words even if she'd tried.

She'd be thrilled to see even her mother right now. *I'll forgive you,* her mind whispered. *I'll forgive you if you just come back. Please come back.*

But neither of them was coming back. She was completely alone.

She blinked hard and glanced at Shadow. No, not completely alone. Not anymore.

It was time to go. Time to be brave.

Raven unbuttoned her raincoat but left it on. She tugged the hood over her head and hoisted her backpack. She considered using the hoverboard, but decided to wait until she was safely in the woods. The lifting blades made a quiet whirring sound. She needed to be completely silent.

She had what she needed. She would release the animals and then hike for the cabin. There was shelter there. Supplies, including a well and a generator. Solitude. Safety. She could stay there for weeks, months, even longer.

The cabin would be enough. It had to be.

She'd lose the security of the months-worth of food in the storage buildings. But there was nothing she could do about that. She couldn't take the Headhunters on by herself. Not if she wanted to live.

And she did want to live. Even if the infection was burning up her insides, even if the Hydra virus was there inside her, just waiting to show itself—even then. The Headhunters couldn't win. They couldn't have her. And they couldn't have Haven.

"Come on, Shadow." She rose to her feet and wove between the trees. She didn't hear Shadow move, but when she reached the gate, he was right behind her.

Warily, she scanned the grounds. The fog lay white and dense as a stifling blanket, deadening sound. She could see less than thirty feet in any direction. Her pulse rushed in her ears, her breath shallow and panting.

There were no lights. No shadowy figures.

All was clear.

She unlocked the gate with a press of her palm and opened it wide for the hybrids. She stepped through to the second gate and opened that one as well.

Shadow regarded her curiously, tail half-raised.

She gestured to him. "You're free now."

He made up his mind quickly. He trotted through the gates, sniffing the ground eagerly, taking in all the new, strange scents. His ears pricked, and he turned back toward the enclosure, letting out a series of low yips.

A moment later, Luna appeared out of the mist like a white

ghost. She paused at the first gate, hesitating. Shadow yipped to her again, tail low and gently waving.

Luna whined, ears flattening.

Shadow loped to her and nuzzled her neck with his muzzle. He strode a few yards past the gate and turned, looking over his shoulder with that same encouraging gaze he'd given to Raven.

Luna's tail lifted. She took a hesitant step outside the enclosure. She lifted her head, sniffing, ears rising tentatively.

Reassured that Luna would follow in her own time, Shadow bounded off joyfully toward the bears. Luna moved slowly, warily, investigating every scent and object before moving on, heading toward the center of the park—the walk-in enclosure with the lake and the flamingos.

Raven watched them go, a sinking sensation in the pit of her stomach. She hadn't really believed they would follow her around like faithful companions, like dogs. But the deep, wrenching disappointment surprised her. What had she expected?

No time to pity herself now. There was too much to do.

Raven went to the timber wolves' paddock next. On a normal night, they would be locked in their night house. But this was no normal night. Even through the mist, she could see them in the center of their clearing, sitting on their haunches, heads thrown back as they howled their sorrow at the sky. The hairs on her arms lifted.

She unlocked the gates and flung them open. Suki, Loki, and Aspen were the only ones left. She scanned the grounds for the bodies of the other three. She spotted a patch of blood gleaming in the moonlight. The bodies were gone.

The Headhunters must have shorted out the electrified top wires of the fence with a large branch, then climbed inside to retrieve the dead wolves. But for what? For meat? Or something else?

"The cage is open," she whispered, ignoring the pain in her chest. She couldn't think about the dead. She had to focus on the living. "Come on, Suki. Let's go, Loki. I'm sorry for your pack. But it's time to go."

Her brain told her she should feel fear, but she didn't. Not after her terrifying night with the hybrids. Compared to them, the timber wolves seemed practically tame. They knew her, had known her father.

Still, caution was needed. *Don't be stupid*, her dad used to say. *Stupid gets you killed every time.*

She pulled the gate full circle against the fence so that it made a triangular shape with Raven inside it. It wasn't much protection, but the wolves had more important matters to deal with than bothering with her—like escape.

And escape they did. Loki and Aspen galloped out of the enclosure. They took off in the direction of the lodge—or maybe it was the meat in the storage building they smelled.

Only shy, meek Suki remained inside. She whimpered, lowering her body inches from the ground, her tail curled beneath her.

"It's okay," Raven murmured soothingly. She remembered long nights cradling Suki's tiny, shivering form against her own chest for warmth, remembered all those hours spent bottle feeding her, formula dripping down her hands. Sometimes, Suki had suckled the milk from her fingers, her tiny teeth pricking Raven's skin.

Suki inched closer, whining pathetically. Something dark stained her muzzle. Blood. Maybe she'd nuzzled Echo or Titus as they died. Or maybe it was from the rat she'd caught earlier.

"Come on, girl. Come on."

But Suki wouldn't come. Her whine deepened into a frantic, bewildered growl. The wolf was confused, petrified, responding to her terror with aggression.

No matter what Raven tried, she couldn't coax Suki from the enclosure. After several minutes, she gave up. She had too many tasks tonight. She couldn't force Suki to leave her paddock. She could only hope the wolf would work up the courage to escape.

She crept to the bear habitat as the bleak mist slowly enveloped everything. Kodiak and Sage were napping. They looked like great black humps in the gray murk. She quietly opened the service door and then the night house drop gate, careful not to wake them. They'd figure it out on their own when they awoke in an hour or so.

After the bears, she went to the bonobos. They hooted and hollered, swinging enthusiastically from their rope netting when they saw her. Gizmo puffed up his chest, grabbed a handful of excrement, and threw it at her. It struck the viewing window with a splat and oozed down the glass.

He huffed a hoarse, goofy laugh, grinning in delight.

"Classy, Gizmo," she muttered as she opened the metal door inside their night house.

Bonobos weren't as strong or as aggressive as chimps, but they could be dangerous without meaning to, though the girls had never shown any inclination toward violence, and Newton was the calmest of the bunch.

Gizmo, though, was the excitable one. She repeated the same procedure, opening the door fully and backing herself into the space between the wall and the door.

Like the wolves, the bonobos were much more interested in escape than her. Gizmo was the first to leave, whooping to the others as he scampered out onto the path. Pepper and Newton quickly followed, with Zephyr, older and slower, taking up the rear. All four of them charged the snack house, hooting joyously. They'd spent years watching humans relish delectable treats; they were determined to obtain some for themselves.

Raven opened Hera's cage, though her wings were clipped. She opened the door to the otters' habitat, too. There was a river less than three miles away, though she doubted the otters would be able to find it. But she couldn't worry about that now.

She freed the tortoises, the ostriches. Maybe it made her an awful person, but she left Winston the boa constrictor where he was.

The porcupines, Duke and Duchess, waddled toward her in outraged fury when she dared to invade their paddock. They turned their backsides toward her in warning, wiggling their gleaming, sharpened quills. She exited swiftly, door open, leaving them to their own devices.

She circled to the western side of the park, freeing Sal, the zebra; the foxes, who scurried between her legs and streaked to freedom; and Electra, who only gave her a moody stare from her perch atop a faux-rock outcropping, her black-fringed ears flicking grumpily.

And then there was only one animal left.

21

The fog thickened, shrouded the buildings in a funeral veil —like death, settling in to wait. Raven shook her head to clear it. She was letting the fog get to her, letting her imagination run wild. She braced herself, took a breath.

She'd reached the tiger house.

She approached Vlad's enclosure with trepidation, doubt and indecision roaring through her mind. Was she really going to let loose a tiger? Over five hundred pounds of coiled muscle and brute strength. Two-inch fangs. Four-inch claws like blades, built for eviscerating prey.

Was she insane?

If she left him, he would die of thirst and starvation, if he wasn't murdered by the Headhunters first. If she released him...she'd be releasing a lethal apex predator into the world. A predator blessed with a fierce, formidable intelligence.

But maybe the world needed a lethal predator. One who could hunt the Headhunters. Or at least, distract them enough so the other animals—and Raven—could escape. The battle in her mind warred back and forth.

In countries where the people respected tigers and kept their distance, tiger attacks had been rare. It was always humans who had hunted them, taunted them, wounded them, and then reacted with stunned outrage when a tiger responded with violence.

Tigers were wary of humans and usually showed no preference for human meat. Although humans were relatively easy prey, they were not a desired source of food. Most man-eating tigers were old, infirm, or had missing teeth. They chose human victims out of desperation.

Vlad stretched out on his favorite rock, gazing at her with his sharp eyes, tail twitching. *Well?* He seemed to say. *Get on with it.*

First, she made sure the sliding gate Vlad used to enter his chamber from the enclosure was closed. Then she swung the service door wide. She climbed atop the tiger house, using the flimsy maple tree to get her far enough up to grasp the top edge and haul herself up with a grunt. Everything was harder with the pack weighing her down.

From the safety of the tiger house, she looked down at Vlad. "Don't make me regret this."

With her father's SmartFlex, she could open the sliding gate remotely. She swiped the SmartFlex, bypassing apps until she found the one she needed. She flicked the manual override. The gate creaked as it slid open.

Vlad just stared at her.

She twisted and scanned the park again. Still no lights, no human noises, no Headhunters. No one was out searching for her. Whoever Damien really was, he'd kept his word. He hadn't betrayed her.

She whistled one long note, two short. The signal for food. Vlad rose languidly, leapt from his rock, and stalked to his chamber. How long would it take him to figure out the service door was open?

She didn't have long to wait. Within seconds, Vlad sauntered out of the service door like he was embarking on his evening stroll. He raised his great head and stared straight up at her. Their gazes locked.

He was magnificent. And he was terrifying.

She stopped breathing. Adrenaline spiked through her veins. Every hair on her body prickled. From the park side, the roof of the tiger house was only ten feet from the ground. A tiger could leap twelve feet straight up from a dead stand-still.

If he wanted to, Vlad could be on her in less than three seconds. No tranquilizer dart in the world took effect that fast.

He shook his head, tail twitching, as if considering how hungry he was.

"You know me," she said softly. "Who else gives you jerky and back rubs? Who else hangs out with you for hours atop your tiger house? You *know* me."

His ears pricked, listening to her. He gave a loud chuff, whirled, and stalked away.

The enormous tiger vanished into the fog like a specter in the night. As she stared after him, Raven couldn't shake the feeling that she'd either saved them all or made the gravest error of her life.

22

The glint of a flashlight snagged the corner of Raven's eye. She froze.

Moments ago, she'd slipped from the tiger house. Now she was headed for the back gate to open it for the animals. Once she turned off the electrified top wires, the tiger, zebra, and the wolves could leap the wrought-iron fence at any point along the perimeter. The bears and bonobos could clamber over it, while the foxes—Zoe, Zelda, and Magnus—and the otters could squeeze through the bars. The other animals would have to find the open gate to get out.

The fog drifted, impossibly sluggish, an opaque white haze. She knew every loose flagstone in every path of Haven by heart. Yet in the misty darkness, it took on an eerie other-worldliness that prickled the hairs on the back of her neck.

Walking through the fog gave her the eerie sensation of sinking into something deep, impenetrable, alien and unknown.

A scuffling sound came from behind her.

She swung around, peering into the fog. To her right, the reptile house loomed. To her left rose the snack shack, a maple tree growing beside it, its leaves almost gone, bare branches raking the sky.

If someone was out here and had a light, they'd turned it off.

She turned back, kept walking, her footfalls muffled.

She stilled. Was there another footfall, just after hers?

She spun around again, gut clenching. She couldn't see more than fifteen feet in any direction. Distance was impossible to measure. The world outside her circle of visibility might have vanished, and she would never know. She listened for sounds, heard only her own ragged breathing.

She'd never escape at this rate. She was letting the fog get to her, letting her own fear control her.

Raven braced herself, straightened her shoulders. She tucked her tranq gun in her waistband and grasped her rifle, finger curled around the trigger. She resumed walking.

Something dropped directly in front of her.

Raven resisted the urge to leap back in terror, to scream. She remained still, clenching her fists, her teeth. A blurred shape leered out of the murky shadows.

A bonobo materialized. He hooted at her, jumping up and down in glee. His lips peeled back from his teeth as he smiled, his licorice-black eyes glittering eagerly up at her.

"Gizmo," Raven said in relief. "Go terrorize someone else, would you?"

He reached out his leathery fingers—not gesturing for food, but to hold her hand. For a moment, he clasped her fingers gently in his. She stroked the black fur on the back of his hand.

He hopped on one foot, hooted softly, and gave her that hoarse, goofy laugh of his.

Her eyes pricked. "You're free now. Go. Find your troop. Live a good life."

Gizmo rose on his hind legs. His smile changed—his lip curled up, revealing all of his top teeth. To the untrained eye, Gizmo still looked like he was smiling. He wasn't.

It was a fear grin.

She heard the footsteps too late.

A gunshot shattered the air.

Gizmo let out a tortured shriek.

She pivoted, lifting her rifle, finger already starting to squeeze the trigger. Too late. A hand clamped around her mouth. Something knocked the rifle out of her hands, seized her and shoved her back against something hard—a man's chest. The cold muzzle of a gun kissed her temple.

"Don't scream," Jagger said in his harsh, rasping voice. His hot breath scalded her cheek. He stank of sweat and beer. The sour stench of him clogged her nostrils. "Or maybe do."

Her heart jerked, bucking against her ribcage, filling her chest with molten panic. She tried to wrench free, but his grip was iron.

"You got her," a second voice said. A figure materialized out of the fog a few yards to her right.

"You bastard," she hissed.

Damien smiled tightly, his eyes in shadow. He gripped a handgun with two hands, held low, his semi-automatic slung over his shoulder. "That's me."

"We've been looking for you," Jagger said. "And to think, we practically gave up on finding you. Ryker and Cerberus will both be thrilled."

At her feet, Gizmo writhed in agony, his hands clutching his stomach, blood oozing between his fingers, his small black face contorted in pain and confusion. In his entire life, a human had never hurt him.

Damien stood over him, aimed his gun, and shot the bonobo in the head. Gizmo's furred body slumped and went still.

A cold fury rose within Raven. Gizmo was only here because he wanted to greet her, to perform his usual antics, to show off, maybe even to say thank you and goodbye.

Instead, Damien killed him.

"You didn't have to do that!" she cried in a strangled voice. "He wouldn't have hurt anybody!"

Jagger toed the dead ape with his boot, his gun still pressed to the side of her head. "Too bad we can't get a pelt out of this thing."

Somewhere to the east, invisible in the heavy fog, another bonobo wailed in grief. It was Zephyr, Gizmo's mother. Bonobo mother-son pairs were closely bonded for life. She must have seen what happened from a perch on the reptile house roof or one of the elms lining the path.

Zephyr wailed again. She knew what it meant—her son's body lying limp and still. Raven felt the bonobo's pain like her own, stitched into her bones.

"Get that thing to shut up, would you?" Jagger said.

Damien holstered his handgun and grabbed the semi-automatic. He swung and pointed into the fog, firing off several random shots.

"Stop it!" She tried again to wrestle from Jagger's grip. She kicked backward at his shins, clawed at his skinny forearm. "Leave her be! You don't have to kill them!"

Jagger only laughed, an ugly, guttural sound. "They're glorified rodents. Foul, filthy beasts. We're doing them a favor."

She choked on helpless anger, unable to speak.

Damien lowered his semi-automatic and peered into the murk, frowning at the sound of tiny nails scrabbling over a metal roof as Zephyr scurried to safety, still shrieking in anguish.

"Now, let's get down to business," Jagger said in her ear, his breath hot on her cheek. "You the one who let the damn monkeys out?"

"They're not monkeys, they're apes, you moron," she spat, finding her voice.

An ear-splitting yowl echoed through the night. It sounded both close and directionless. A harsh, guttural bark answered from somewhere nearby.

Jagger went rigid. In his shock, his right arm dropped, the gun slipping from her temple. "What the hell was that?"

Damien spun, gun up, sighting nebulous shapes in the shifting fog. He shot Raven a horrified look. "Which animals did you let out?"

"All of them." She let the tremble creep into her voice, let the panic clawing up her throat escape. "That yowl you heard? That's Vlad, the man-eating tiger. It's the sound he makes right before he attacks."

It was a lie. The yowl was Electra's, the dog-like bark belonged to the zebra—neither of whom would attack three full-grown adults. But Jagger and Damien didn't know that.

Their faces drained of color. Jagger's attention strayed from Raven to the menacing fog, which hid any number of clawed, fanged, and deadly creatures.

"Where is it?" he cried. "Shoot, damn it, shoot!"

Damien crouched, his gaze sweeping in a slow circle. "I don't see anything!"

Jagger gestured with his gun. "Shoot anyway! Scare it!"

Raven saw her moment and took it. She threw herself backward, slamming into Jagger's chest to loosen his one-armed grip. The quarters were too close for the rifle. Instead, she shoved her hand into her pocket and seized the whittling knife. She yanked it out, fumbling to flip it open.

She didn't think. She simply acted in desperate self-preservation. Carnivores always went for the most vulnerable points of the body—and so did she.

Raven twisted, arm raised, and plunged the blade deep into Jagger's throat.

23

Hot blood drenched Raven's hands, slicked her fingers. The knife slipped out of her hands and clattered to the flagstone.

Jagger staggered back. His face went slack with astonishment. He dropped his gun. His eyes were sunken in his gaunt face, his pallor ashen. He clutched his neck with both hands, frantically trying—and failing—to staunch the dark red blood gushing from the wound.

"Shoot her!" he croaked.

Damien's wide gaze darted from Jagger to Raven and back again. His expression was stony, his shoulders clenched. He swung his semi-automatic toward her, gun barrel pointed at her chest. "Raise your hands."

The knife lay on the path, dark with blood, a yard from her feet, Jagger's gun even further away. Her hunting rifle was still slung over her shoulder, but by the time she went for it, Damien could shoot her a dozen times.

"Raise your hands!" Damien said again.

She went very quiet and very still. She lifted both blood-drenched hands in the air and fixed her gaze on Damien. "You don't have to do this."

Jagger took a step toward her and stumbled, gasping, half-choking. "What're you waiting for? Kill her!"

"You have a choice," Raven said to Damien.

Jagger tottered backward, hands fumbling, plucking at the spurting hole in his neck. He sank to his knees. His breath came in shallow, rapid pants. "Kill her and get me to Gomez! He's got the med kit..."

Still, Damien hesitated. His rifle wavered. His body was taut, his expression guarded, calculating. His gaze flitted from Jagger to Raven and back again. Something flashed in his eyes—uncertainty.

Blood bubbled from Jagger's lips. His skin had lost all color. He made an attempt to stand but toppled to the ground with a groan.

His hands tightened over his throat, blood still gushing from the wound, spreading in a thick, shining black puddle. "I'll kill...you myself...you little—"

"No," Damien said firmly, his expression clearing like he'd decided something. He shifted and aimed his rifle at Jagger. "You won't."

Damien didn't pull the trigger. He didn't need to.

Jagger sputtered incoherently. He gasped for air, making choking, gurgling noises, his eyes rolling back in his head. Raven forced herself to watch, dismayed, horrified—but alive.

Within a minute, Jagger stopped moving, stopped breathing, stopped everything.

He was dead.

Damien lowered the semi-automatic, but he kept his finger on the trigger. His breathing was ragged, his face hard. "You were supposed to run," he said, his voice accusatory.

"I *was*. Until *you* caught me."

"That was...out of my control."

She bared her teeth. "You were there. I saw you. You were shooting at the wolves. Shika, Echo, and Titus are dead."

A shadow crossed his face. "I had no choice."

She choked out a furious, disbelieving snort.

"I shot *at* them—I didn't kill them myself."

"You might as well have." She wiped her hands fiercely on her cargo pants, leaving dark streaks of blood. "And Gizmo? What's your pathetic excuse for murdering him?"

"Jagger shot him first. I put him out of his misery, and you know it."

In some small part of her brain, she knew Damien's shot was a mercy killing. He'd ended Gizmo's suffering. All the same, she hated him with a blazing intensity. Seeing him standing there next to Ryker and Cerberus while they killed Shika and Titus and Echo—it had felt like a betrayal. "You nearly killed Phil."

"I was *saving* him—from Ryker. Ryker would have killed him too if I hadn't stepped in. I never would have shot that old man." He ran a hand through his hair and sighed. "Look, I can't act weak, okay? I have to play a part. If I don't, they'll abandon me—or kill me."

"So what? Just leave."

"It's not that easy or simple."

"Looks that easy from where I'm standing."

His gaze dropped to Jagger's body, and swiftly snapped up again. "Cerberus is my uncle, okay?"

She just stared at him.

"He came for me." His voice was strained, his eyes hooded. "I was stuck in my house for five days, afraid to leave with all the rioting and bloodlust, people so scared, they killed anyone who coughed or breathed wrong—some who didn't even do that. I was in that house with my dead parents and my dead sisters for five days."

He didn't look at her, didn't meet her gaze. He stared off into the mist, eyes glazed and distant, recalling the horror. "I thought I was going to die too, just like them, the fevers, the coughing up blood, writhing in agony, my insides melting like jelly. But I didn't. I'm immune." His voice went hollow. "Lucky me."

"I'm sorry," she said, because she could see the suffering etched on his face, sharpening his features.

"And then Cerberus came," Damien said. "He fought his way through a riot and dragged me out of that house and he saved me. So I'm alive because of him. I owe him."

"He sounds like a real winner."

"He's—he's not as bad as you think. He has a code. He doesn't usually kill women and children."

Her eyebrows shot to her hairline, incredulous. "Usually?"

Damien's eyes flashed, going hard again. "Trust me. There are worse alternatives."

She remembered the look on Ryker's face, his flat eyes as he blew Carl's face off for no reason but mild irritation. Damien had a point.

She scowled. The Headhunters were killers and criminals and thugs. Every single one of them. "Do you think any of that matters to Carl? To Echo or Gizmo?"

His jaw pulsed. Emotions flitted across his face—anger, resignation, something like sadness. "I'm not your enemy."

He lifted both hands, releasing his rifle, palms out in a token of trust, maybe—which she didn't believe for a second. She couldn't allow herself to believe it.

She didn't trust him. She despised him. He was one of them. Yet he'd been true to his word. He hadn't ratted her out back at the lodge.

He'd also stood by and watched his wicked friends shoot the wolves. He'd done nothing when Jagger took her hostage. Yet he'd refused to shoot her, choosing to allow one of his own people to die instead.

It made no sense. She didn't understand it, didn't understand him. His presence was disorienting, discomfiting, filling her with anxiety and apprehension.

His hands were off his rifle. She could reach hers, lift, point, and shoot. Maybe she'd get a shot off before he did. He was a Headhunter. He was dangerous.

She should kill him right now.

24

Raven reached for her weapon.

Damien tensed, but he didn't move. He kept his hands up, palms out. "Are you going to do it, then?"

She should. She needed to. Her father would have.

But there was something in his eyes. A softness, a vulnerability. Her gut twisted. He was the enemy. He'd also spared her life. Twice.

She could hate him, but she couldn't kill him. With a sigh, she released the rifle. "Why didn't you shoot me when Jagger told you too?"

"I told you, I'm not a killer."

But you are. She pressed her trembling hands against her thighs. They wouldn't stop shaking. "And yet I still find that hard to believe."

"I'm just trying to survive like everybody else. That doesn't mean I like what I have to do."

She regarded him with narrowed eyes, still wary. "I don't understand you."

He gave a helpless shrug. "I do what I can to help, when I can."

"As long as it doesn't cost you anything."

He glanced away, stiffening, that muscle in his jaw pulsing. He turned and met her gaze. There was an odd look in his eyes. Part angry. Part ashamed. "You're right. I'm a coward."

"Then we agree on something."

"I guess so." There was no sarcasm or defensiveness in his voice. Only a weary resignation.

A scratching, shuffling sound came from behind them.

Damien went rigid. Raven tensed, holding up one finger. Eyes wide, Damien nodded. He gripped his rifle, pointing aimlessly into the fog.

She strained her ears, trying to make out the source of the sounds. The mist was thick as soup around them—she couldn't see a thing. For a panicked instant, she imagined the tiger stalking them, creeping closer, closer, unsheathed claws clicking the flagstone.

But no. The sounds were wrong.

More heavy, shuffling steps. A low whoof.

A dark shape reared out of the murk behind Damien, a huge looming shadow.

Damien whirled, squeaking in alarm.

"Don't shoot!" Raven hissed. She lunged forward, grasped the barrel of Damien's gun, and slapped it down.

Damien shot her a horrified look.

"Stay still and he won't hurt you."

The enormous black bear emerged from the thick fog. Damien made a strangled sound in the back of his throat.

Kodiak lumbered toward them, his huge head low as he sniffed hungrily at the bushes along the path, searching for potential dinner. His heavy body was thickly furred, all black but for the white, star-shaped patch between his eyes.

He hesitated about ten feet away. He looked at them curiously, small eyes glancing from Damien to Raven. Damien's face was so pale, his freckles stood out like drops of blood.

"Don't move," she murmured. "He's more curious than anything."

The bears were big, lazy oafs. Dangerous, sure, but not aggressive. Not if you knew what you were doing.

"No food here, boy," she said. "Exit's back the way you came."

Kodiak snuffled eagerly and lumbered on, passing not five feet from where she and Damien stood. She could smell the dankness of his fur, make out the individual hairs along his broad back.

Damien stared after the black bear until he vanished into the fog, his mouth slightly opened. He turned back to Raven with a shake of his head. "I thought he was gonna try and eat us."

"Most animals aren't a threat to humans unless the humans are a threat first," she snapped.

He ran his hands through his hair and took a steadying breath. His gaze fell to Jagger's body. His face darkened. "I have to go back and alert Cerberus and Ryker."

She'd dallied here for far too long. Every second she stood here with him increased the chance of discovery. She picked up her knife, wiped it clean on her pants, flicked it closed, and crammed it back in her pocket.

You killed someone with that. Part of her never wanted to see it again. Part of her couldn't bear to leave it. It had saved her life. And it was her mother's last gift to her. "I'm already gone."

"Wait." Damien swiftly crossed the space between them and seized her arm.

"Let go!" She tried to wrench free, feeling his touch like a shudder all the way up her arm. The buzz of fear, the prickle of alarm, but also something else, something she couldn't name, that turned her stomach inside out. Her skin felt too tight, the air too dense.

He was stronger than she was, but he released her arm with a frown.

"What do you want?" she asked harshly.

"There's something you need to know."

The fog thickened around them in a murky white soup. They stood facing each other, tension sizzling between them like electricity. Her muscles were taut, ready to flee at the slightest provocation.

If he touched her again, she was gone.

"They'll hunt you now," he said hoarsely. "They were losing interest, but Ryker won't stop. He's like a dog with a bone."

She stared at him, numb. "It was an accident. Self-defense."

"Do you think they care about that? Do you think Ryker will care? This isn't just anybody." He inhaled sharply. "Jagger is—was—Ryker's brother."

His words sent a frisson of dread down her spine. All the blood rushed to her head. Ryker was dangerous. She'd known it the moment she laid eyes on him back at the pharmacy. The images seared her mind—Carl's face imploding, blood spraying everywhere, Ryker's flat, dead-fish eyes.

Now those eyes would be focused on her. Before, she'd been invisible. She could have left like she'd planned and none of the Headhunters would've been the wiser for it. But now, she would be pursued, stalked, hunted.

Damien's mouth tightened. "You need to understand. Cerberus wanted to take you in alive, before this. It wouldn't matter what Ryker wanted—he'd have to obey. But now he has a blood debt against you. Cerberus won't stop him. Ryker will kill you. And not nicely."

"I got that part."

"Want to know why I was hiding in that back room?" Damien asked.

She glanced at him.

He shook his head as if angry at himself, again not meeting her gaze. "Because I felt like I couldn't breathe anymore in there, with them. Every time Ryker looks at me, I don't know if he's gonna smile that slick, sly smile of his or slide a blade between my ribs. He sees me as a threat because of who I am to Cerberus. He'd take over if he thought he could get away with it. He's dangerous, is what I'm trying to say."

She nodded and licked her dry lips. Her scalp prickled with cold sweat. "I'll hide the body—"

"There's blood all over the flagstone."

"They'll think it was one of the wild animals. The tiger or one of the bears."

"Even I know animals leave a carcass behind." He grimaced. "I have no choice. I have to tell Ryker. If I don't, they'll discover the body anyway and he'll suspect me, too. He knows Jagger and I went out together."

Impotent rage filled her. At Damien, at the Headhunters, at her dead father, her mother who wasn't here, who'd left her all alone, at this whole stupid sick and dying world.

"You have to get out of here," Damien said.

Once again, she found herself running for her life.

25

Raven fled.

She ran and ran, her legs pumping, her pack thumping against her spine, her pulse a roar in her ears. Tears burned her vision. She blinked them away fiercely.

She sprinted between the bear and hybrid paddocks, nearly tripping over one of the peacocks that veered into her path, finally reaching the wide double gates at the back of Haven Wildlife Refuge.

She pressed her palm to the bioscanner to unlock the security panel. She swiped the buttons, opening the gates and disengaging the electrified wires along the entire exterior perimeter fence.

The gates creaked open.

The forest was a black wall before her—bleak, foreboding, full of terrors.

Voices echoed behind her. The Headhunters. They would find Jagger's body soon. And then they would come for her.

She hesitated for the barest moment, glancing back over her

shoulder, peering through the fog. *Come on, Shadow. Come on, Luna.* And Vlad, Suki, Kodiak, all the others. She couldn't wait for them. She had to trust that they could find their way out.

She ran into the woods. Burrs and brambles clung to her clothing, thorns snagged her hands. The underbrush was thick and dense. The woods smelled of crushed pine needles and damp, dark earth.

The moon glimmered between black tangles of branches. The skeletons of the trees stretched long bony fingers to scrape the sky.

The darkness closed around her like a fist.

She kept her eyes open wide, wary of every flicker of movement, every sigh of the leaves, every pulsing shadow in the underbrush. A second of inattention determined the difference between living and dying. A single wrong move—tripping on a tree root, stepping wrong on a felled branch, brushing too loudly against a bush, bumping into a tree and rattling its leaves—would alert predators to her presence.

Brambles, burrs, and thorns tore at her pant legs and jacket sleeves, snagged on her boots and laces, seeking the tender skin of her hands and neck as she moved, swiftly but carefully, shadows spilling all around her like ink.

Sweat beaded her forehead and dripped between her shoulder blades, her muscles strung taut. Her every footfall, no matter how precise and careful she tried to be, announced her presence to the night, to all the creatures that called this wild forest their home—and to some that did not.

Raven searched the darkness for shifting shadows, for the gleam of predatory eyes. She strained for the sound of padded paws slinking through the forest, creeping closer, closer, while she was effectively stumbling blind.

A flash of silver streaked through the trees on her right. A twig cracked on her left. She halted, going completely still, gripping the rifle.

Ten yards away, Luna stepped between two trees. Shadow glided up beside her, a shadow among shadows. Raven crouched against a large log. Relief flooded every cell of her body. Wetness blurred her eyes. She choked it back.

"You came back for me," she whispered. "You came back."

Shadow brushed his powerful shoulder against hers. Knocked off balance, she fell back against the log. Her pack took the brunt of the impact. She grunted, tried to rise, but abruptly her legs were like water.

She looked down at her trembling hands. Blood stained her fingers. Blood from a dead man.

And then the weight of it struck her, unbearably heavy, like a thousand bricks pressed against her chest. She'd just killed a human being. With her own two hands.

She was a killer. A murderer.

No. It was self-defense. Like every wild creature, she'd instinctively protected herself. The drive for self-preservation was innate. Still, the brutal images crashed through her mind—the plunge of the knife, slick in her hands; the wound gaping open like a raw, red mouth; Jagger's stunned expression, eyes going wide; the blood spraying, gurgling from his throat as he gasped for breath.

She leaned over and vomited.

Shaking, she wiped her mouth with the back of her hand.

She had to pull herself together. She couldn't stay here. She needed to get to the safety of the cabin. Then she could fall apart.

She took several steadying breaths and glanced at Shadow. He was watching her, ears pricked, tail swishing slowly. She managed a grim smile. "You have no idea how happy I am to see you."

Gradually, her mind-numbing terror faded. Now that the wolves were here, she felt immeasurably better.

She had never been afraid of the dark or of these woods. But tonight, surrounded by predators of all kinds, the last thing she wanted to be was alone.

Would the wolves follow her? She almost didn't dare to hope. She wasn't sure she could bear the profound disappointment—of loss—if the wolves left her again. She felt stronger just being in their presence. Braver.

She dug inside one of the outside compartments of her pack and withdrew three strips of dried venison. She gnawed on a strip herself and tossed a piece to each of them. Shadow sniffed his, unconvinced.

She took a long swallow from her water bottle and wiped her mouth. "It's good, I promise."

He licked it, gave a little whine, then wolfed it down in one gulp. Luna sniffed hers daintily and lifted her nose in disdain. Shadow happily ate her share.

Luna and Shadow regarded her, their heads tilted, as if asking, *what now?*

"The cabin," she said, climbing to her feet. "There's more jerky where that came from. But you have to come with me."

Shadow's ears flattened. Luna growled low in her throat.

Raven froze, her hands going to the rifle.

Simultaneously, both wolves whirled and bolted into the darkness.

She was alone again. She shivered against the chill snaking cold fingers around her neck. She could do it alone if she had to. She was used to it, after all. They would come back. They'd found her once. They could do it again.

A wave of dizziness flashed through her. She fought it off. The adrenaline from the fight was wearing off. She was incredibly weary. Her eyes burned. She couldn't remember the last time she'd slept.

Something rustled behind her.

She spun around, heart clenching. "Shadow?"

And then she heard them, crashing through the underbrush, grunting and swearing. A gunshot went off. Then another.

The Headhunters.

26

The hairs on Raven's arms lifted, her scalp prickling. Something—or someone—was close. She could feel it. She didn't have time to run.

She scanned the forest, looking for a place to hide. Near the roots of the fallen tree, a sliver of space gapped between trunk and earth, no taller than a foot. It was enough.

The Headhunters crashed and blundered behind her. They were big and clumsy in the dark, but they were also strong, angry, and well-armed.

She scrambled over the side of the log and burrowed in the deep underbrush growing along its flank, managing to jam most of her body beneath the log, the rifle butt jammed against her shoulder, the barrel digging into her thigh. Except for her pack. Swiftly, she reached up and bent a few low branches of an oak leaf hydrangea, covering herself and the pack with its reddish-purple leaves.

The gnarled roots of the tree rose in pale and tangled knots above her. A centipede crawled beneath the sleeve of her jacket, onto her bare arm. Something else crawled along her ankle. She stilled, inhaling the decaying scent of dead leaves, the sharp scent of pine.

If the Headhunters took the easy path, bypassing the log, they would miss her.

Nearby, another twig cracked. A bush rustled. Something was moving only ten yards downwind of her. She steadied her breathing, sure whatever it was could hear her thumping heartbeat. *Disappear. Disappear.*

And then the Headhunters were upon her. They crashed into the small clearing, breathing hard, cursing.

"You find anything, Ryker?" Cerberus asked.

"Found some footprints a ways back," Ryker said, his voice so close she flinched. "If it wasn't so dark and damn foggy..."

She hadn't even heard Ryker. He must have been the source of the rustling sound she'd heard—he'd gotten far too close for comfort.

"We'll find her," Scorpio said. "She can't have gone far."

Ryker's voice was filled with raw fury. "No one touches her but me."

"Don't worry," Cerberus said. "You'll avenge your brother. I'll make sure of it."

Raven closed her eyes.

"You positive you don't got any idea which way she went?" Scorpio asked gruffly. She could hear him stomping around the underbrush a few yards from where she hid.

"I told you," Damien said, sounding frustrated and defensive. "As soon as I went to help Jagger, she took off. I didn't see anything."

"I found blood on a leaf forty yards back." Ryker's voice was low and deadly, sharp-edged as a knife. "My brother's blood."

No one asked him how he knew it was Jagger's blood. They didn't have to.

"We'll keep looking," Cerberus said.

"What about the animals?" someone asked. "She released them all."

"Scorpio already got one of the foxes," Cerberus said. "We want these pelts, we need to get them now, before they scatter. It's hunting season, boys."

"And the tiger?" Damien asked, a hint of unease flickering through his voice. "The bears?"

"We have automatic weapons." Cerberus snorted. "And they're caged beasts trained to bask on fake rocks all day. It'll be like shooting fish in a barrel. Only much more fun."

"Just get me that damn girl," Ryker sneered.

"You're all angry," Cerberus boomed. "You all want blood for Jagger. He was one of us, one of our own. I'll give you that blood!"

Several Headhunters shouted, jeering, cheering.

She heard the cock of a rifle. "Find the girl. Kill everything that moves."

Raven waited, completely still, as the Headhunters broke off into pairs of twos and threes and headed deeper into the woods to hunt.

If she were stealthy, she could still get past them. She knew how to be quiet, how to stay hidden.

But that meant leaving Shadow, Luna, and the others behind. Leaving Zephyr and Suki and Sage to fend for themselves. Her stomach roiled.

Cerberus was right. They'd spent their lives in captivity. They didn't know to fear humans. Kodiak would come right up to them if they offered him food. So would Loki, the other two foxes, even grumpy Electra.

She had to pull herself together. Right now.

She hadn't freed the animals just so the Headhunters could

hunt them down one by one. She rose to her feet, wincing as her muscles ached in protest. She tightened her grip on the rifle.

The Headhunters weren't the only human predators in these woods. Raven was a hunter, too.

27

R aven hunted.

She caked her face and hands with red dirt. She smeared the bottom of her boots and stuck them full of leaves and twigs to mar her footprints. She adjusted the rifle, strapping it over her chest and checked the tranq gun, still tucked into her waistband. She kept the knife folded in her pocket.

The Headhunters were loud. They stumbled and thrashed through the underbrush. If they were hunting wild creatures, they never would have found them. But the captive animals were confused, anxious, and frightened. The alien scents and strange sounds were alarming and disorienting.

The Headhunters began to pick them off. Every few minutes, gunshots shattered the night air. The men shouted to each other through the trees. She heard the retort of a rifle, the rat-a-tat of an automatic weapon.

This wasn't hunting.

It was barbaric. It was a massacre.

It needed to stop.

She snuck up on a man with a craggy face and cinderblock head. He was leaning against an elm tree, peering through his scope at a moving shape she couldn't make out at first.

She glimpsed one of the bonobos, Newton, perched in the lower branches of a red maple, happily tearing scarlet leaves to shreds.

For one agonizing second, she debated whether to shoot the man with the rifle or the tranq gun. He was a Headhunter. He was a bad guy.

Damien's enigmatic face flashed through her mind. He'd helped her twice, for no reason, against every sense of his own self-preservation.

She'd killed a man already tonight. Some deep, weary part of herself couldn't stomach doing it again. But she couldn't simply shoot him with a tranq and allow him to wake up in four hours and continue his killing spree.

She had to do enough to stop them. A cold determination crept over her. Her breathing steadied. Her frantic heartbeat calmed. She would do this.

She would protect what she could of Haven.

She refused to let the Headhunters win.

Raven picked up the rifle, the safety already off, a round chambered, and aimed. She widened her stance, fit the stock against her shoulder, found the target in her sights. She inhaled, exhaled, squeezed the trigger. The bullet struck where she'd aimed it—in the man's hamstring.

The Headhunter shrieked and slammed to his knees. He dropped his gun and twisting, clutching at the back of his leg, gasping from the pain.

Newton screeched in alarm. He scooted up the tree limb and leaped to another tree, scampering off into the darkness.

The Headhunter's partner crashed through the woods toward him.

Raven slunk back between the trees. She got a safe distance from the man's screams, then hunkered down behind a tall stump, waiting and listening for her next target.

She heard two more Headhunters stalking Kodiak, who was loudly lumbering through the underbrush, searching for berries. Before either of them got off a shot, she'd fired two bullets at close range—striking one in the calf, the other in the shoulder.

Screams mingled with the shouts now. Confusion and fear were taking hold. Good. Maybe the Headhunters were ready to give up now. To save their lives, all they had to do was leave.

A low growl sent shivers up her spine. It was close. Too close.

Several yards away, a Headhunter grunted. "Stay back now."

Raven pressed herself against the closest trunk, then edged carefully around it. Five yards away, a Hispanic Headhunter in a brown baseball cap—Gomez—stood facing one of the timber wolves, his rifled aimed at the wolf's head.

The wolf snarled menacingly, back arched, hackles raised. For a moment, she didn't even recognize who it was, so alien was her ferocious snarl. It was meek, shy Suki. She faced down the Headhunter with amber eyes blazing.

"Go on now! Get!" Gomez's hands were shaking. He fired wide, in Suki's direction but not straight at her.

Suki skittered to the side. Raven expected her to flee, but she didn't.

The Headhunter fired again, another wide shot. Bark splintered several feet above Suki's head. She yelped and snarled, but still refused to run.

He wasn't trying to hit her, Raven realized with a start. Damien had been right—they weren't all bloodthirsty killers. This Head-hunter wasn't hunting the wolf—the wolf was attacking him.

Darkened blood matted the fur along Suki's jaw, mingled with a sickly, yellowish saliva. It glistened from her fangs and dripped down her muzzle, staining the white hairs on her chest.

Raven stared at Suki, dread pooling in her stomach. She'd never seen saliva like that. Something was wrong. Very wrong.

Wolves rarely attacked humans, nearly never. They were wary, cautious creatures. If the man had invaded her territory or gone after one of the pack's pups, maybe.

But Suki hadn't been backed into a corner. She could escape. But she wasn't. She'd confronted him. Even after he'd shot at her, she was still snarling, lunging at him, teeth snapping.

"Damn it!" Gomez swore. "You're infected." He fired again, again purposefully missing. "Just back away now. Go!"

Raven stared at Suki's gleaming fangs, bewildered. How could she have gotten infected? Zachariah didn't go inside the enclosure. But her father had. Had he somehow passed the virus on to Suki?

Growling and snapping, Suki sprang at the Headhunter. He dodged, still trying to aim as she hurtled toward him, snapping, then darted away, only to fling herself at him from another angle, again and again.

Gomez cursed. There was no aggression in his face, no hatred—only rank fear. He stumbled back, his rifle flailing wildly.

Raven swung her rifle up, aiming at Gomez. She sighted him in her crosshairs. *Just do it.* But something made her hesitate. He wasn't the danger here. Suki was.

Raven didn't want to shoot either of them.

Suki lunged at the Headhunter. Eighty pounds of fury and fangs struck him in the chest. He fell back. Gomez dropped the rifle, throwing his hands up to protect his face and throat.

Snarling, Suki's muzzle flashed in. Her jaws closed over his forearm.

Gomez howled.

Wolf and man wrestled in a death-lock. Gomez punched Suki's face, but she wouldn't let go. She growled as she sank her powerful jaws deep into his flesh. Raven heard the snap and crunch of pulverizing bone, muscle, tendons.

Gomez fumbled frantically for his holster at his hip, jerked out his gun, and jammed it against Suki's chest.

Raven stood frozen, unsure what to do. She didn't want to shoot this Headhunter. She didn't want to shoot Suki.

If she tried to separate them, Suki would turn on Raven. The wolf was in a blind fury—enraged, infected, deadly.

Gomez pulled the trigger. Once, twice, three times. Suki never even whimpered. She dropped like a sack of grain, instantly dead.

28

A gaping hole opened up deep inside Raven. *No, no, no...*

"Gomez!" another Headhunter shouted. "You okay?"

"I'm fine!" Gomez yelled. With a shudder, he shoved the dead wolf off himself and climbed weakly to his feet. He quickly shrugged off his jacket and slung it over his arm, hiding the bite.

Two Headhunters lumbered through the underbrush. She recognized Oman's thick, bristling beard. He gripped a semi-automatic in both hands, the other guy aiming the flashlight at the ground to light their way. "Did it get you?"

"Nah, man," Gomez said shakily.

Oman nudged Suki's body with his boot. He gave a contemptuous snort. "It's infected. You're lucky. One bite is all it takes. Just like those damn infected dogs."

Gomez leaned against the nearest tree. It was too dark for the other Headhunters to see the tremor in his legs, the stain of blood slowly seeping through his jacket. But Raven saw it all. "I nailed it before it even got near me."

"Good thing," the other Headhunter said, peering into the woods just a few feet from where Raven crouched. She held her breath. "Diaz and Cooper got shot."

"That girl?" Gomez asked, panting.

The second Headhunter turned back to the others. "I'll kill her myself if I find her first."

"I've had enough," Oman growled. "We'll hunt her down when it's light and we can see our hands in front of our faces." He glanced at Gomez. "You coming?"

"Nah—I'll stay out a bit longer," Gomez said. "Found some more tracks. Gonna bag me that lynx."

"Suit yourself," Oman said. "I'll take this one." He slung Suki's body over his shoulders and left, the other thug right behind him.

Gomez sank down to the ground, breathing hard. Raven watched as he unwrapped his bloody jacket and examined his arm. Even in the dim moonlight, she could make out the black blood leaking from the ugly gash of jagged, ripped flesh Suki's jaws had torn in his forearm.

A raw, guttural sob escaped Gomez's throat.

Raven lowered her rifle. Gomez was a dead man walking. *One bite is all it takes*, Oman had said. Now Gomez was infected. The Hydra virus must work differently in animals, making them more aggressive, like rabies, the virus blazing inside them determined to spread itself through bites and saliva.

She still didn't know whether she was infected, too. It had been four days. She felt no scratch in the back of her throat. She'd coughed only a few times. She felt her forehead with her free hand. Her skin was warm, but not hot. No fever had set in—yet.

If death was coming, so be it. Until then, she planned to fight like hell to survive.

Raven backed slowly away, her stomach roiling.

She was done with hunting. She was sick and tired of everything, of sickness and death and violence. Sick of the constant fear wrenching her stomach. Sick of the dried blood on her hands. Sick of the specter of grief always hot on her heels, ready to sink its claws of despair into her the moment she stopped running.

The unfairness of it all made her want to destroy something. Suki had never so much as growled at anyone in her life. She deserved to make it. She should have been one of the survivors.

The Headhunters were gathering their wounded. They'd take their people back to the lodge, attempt to staunch the blood and stitch up their wounds. She doubted they would leave for good. But she'd done what she could.

She'd given the animals a night to escape, to disappear deep into the woods, to find a way to survive. It would have to be enough.

With a resigned sigh, she checked the compass on the Smart-Flex. She headed northwest, toward the cabin.

The back of her neck prickled. A sigh in the wind, a flicker in the shadows. Something made her look down.

Sunk into the dirt, surrounded by scattered leaves, was a single, perfect paw print. A pad and four toes, spanning over five inches wide.

Only one animal could make that distinctive mark.

Tiger.

29

Raven didn't get far. Within minutes, her weariness overtook her. Her steps became sloppy, breaking twigs and bending leaves, making far more sound than she should, leaving a trail for the Headhunters to follow.

She considered switching to the hoverboard, but she was afraid that in her exhaustion, she'd fall right off. She couldn't keep going. She had to find a safe place to rest.

She had her tarp, tent, and sleeping bag, but the thought of Vlad close by, prowling through the misty darkness made her think twice about bedding down on the ground.

Maybe a tree? Tigers could climb, but they didn't particularly like to. It was probably her safest bet. She had a rope. She could find a large oak with a thick branch twenty-five or so feet off the ground. She could tie herself to the branch to keep from falling and breaking her neck.

She walked for several more minutes, straining to see further than a dozen feet, still afraid to switch on a light. The Headhunters had abandoned the forest—for now. The night sounds had returned:

crackling branches, the hoot of an owl, the raspy song of crickets and cicadas.

She found a suitable tree and was shrugging off her pack to find the rope when she sensed something behind her.

Her heart jolted, adrenaline shooting through her veins. She remained still, outwardly calm, and turned slowly.

Luna stood beside a fallen log, white as the ghostly mist swirling around her paws.

Raven dropped to her knees. Instinctively, she bowed her head, though it made her feel a bit ridiculous. She didn't care. Overwhelming relief flooded through her. "I can't tell you how happy I am to see you."

Luna's lips pulled up, just enough to show a sliver of teeth. But she pivoted and trotted north, gliding between a gnarled pine tree and a tall thicket of thorns. Just before she slipped out of sight, she paused, looking back over her shoulder. Just like Shadow last night.

An invitation. She wanted Raven to follow her.

Raven rose, re-shouldered her pack, and obeyed. "Please don't go far, or my feet will fall off."

She trailed Luna for almost a mile, winding through dense thickets of mountain laurel and sumac, traipsing through copses of yellowwood, maple, and white oak trees. Luna would disappear, loping much too swiftly for Raven to keep up.

Raven stopped and waited. A few minutes later, Luna reappeared, her lips slightly pulled back, not a snarl but possibly a grimace, her expression looking for all the world like an irritated mother.

"I'm trying," Raven grunted. Her legs ached. Her eyes burned. Exhaustion pressed down on her like the weight of the sky.

Luna led her up a steep hill, around several moss-covered boulders that reared out of the fog like monstrous beasts, setting Raven's heart aflutter.

Luna paused again before a massive rock jutting at least fifteen feet high and twenty feet across. She ducked and slipped inside a dark crevice at its base. A cave.

A series of yips and whines echoed from inside the cave. Shadow emerged, tail wagging. He trotted right up to Raven and pushed his shoulder against her hip in what she recognized now as a sign of greeting, maybe even of affection.

"Hello to you, too." She reached out and gently grazed the ruff of his neck. He didn't growl or react.

Growing bolder, she dared to stroke his back. Though his guard hairs were coarse, the fur was soft underneath.

Shadow circled her, rubbing against her thighs as she petted him, nearly knocking her off her feet. He trotted to the cave entrance, ducked his head, and entered.

For a long moment, Raven stood alone in the darkness, debating what to do.

In the wild, adult wolves didn't use dens unless they had pups, preferring to sleep outside beneath the stars. Was it possible they chose this cave for her?

Did they want her to come inside with them? Was that why they'd invited her here? If they didn't want her, her invasion of such a tight, intimate space could trigger a defensive attack.

She had two options. Find another tree and spend an exhausted, restless night freezing cold and incredibly uncomfortable? Or accept the invitation of these strange, wild creatures and willingly enter a wolves' den?

She chose the wolves.

Raven crept to the crevice, careful to keep her balance on the sharp, slippery edges of the rocky shelf. She removed her pack and hid it behind a smaller boulder, quickly cutting a few slender branches from a nearby pine with her knife and covering the pack completely.

Before she crawled into the cave, she took a few pieces of jerky and a handful of nuts from her pack and ate tiredly. Though she was thirsty, she took only a few swallows of water from her water bottle. She needed to conserve what remained.

Inside the cave, it was dark and smelled of earth, pine, and rotting leaves. She flicked on her SmartFlex flashlight. The cave was maybe six feet across and four feet high, narrowing into a small tunnel at the back. On the far left side, Shadow and Luna lay together. Shadow licked Luna's muzzle while she nuzzled her head against his neck.

Raven curled up on the rocky ground as far to the right as she could, giving the wolves their space while still facing the entrance. She shivered, unable to get warm. She pressed the back of her hand to her forehead. Still no fever. But her throat was dry and hurt when she swallowed. Was that a symptom? She couldn't remember. She was too tired to worry about it now.

Raven flicked off the light, the rifle by her side, the knife in her hand. She wasn't necessarily afraid of the wolves, but she *was* concerned another wild creature might find this cave a suitable shelter. Or a Headhunter still out there, searching for her.

She fought to keep her eyes open, determined to remain alert.

Her eyelids grew heavier and heavier. She breathed in the warm dankness of the cave, the sweetly sour scent of wolf, and watched the darkness beyond the cave entrance blur and fade.

30

Sometime in the night, Raven awoke with a start.

For an instant, she had no idea where she was, or why. Her limbs were stiff and achy, the rocky ground cold and hard.

Something huge and hot and hairy pressed up against her side. Something equally warm—and heavy—lay across her legs.

She reached out in the dark. Felt fur, heat, the rise and fall of steady breathing.

Her pulse quickened. In the dim starlight trickling from the cave entrance, she could just make out Luna's pale shape sleeping beside her. The dark form of Shadow sprawled across her shins.

His head was down, resting on his forelegs, but his eyes were open. Keeping watch, protecting them, protecting his pack.

Emotion surged within her: a trembling astonishment, a deep, radiating awe and wonder. The world was unbearably broken, but it also held an unbearably fragile beauty.

Gradually, awe deepened to something else, something akin to a profound contentment. Even in the midst of everything. In that moment, she felt...at peace.

It was like nothing she'd felt in a long, long time. Maybe ever.

It was comfort. It was connection.

Her father had spent hours and hours by her side: deep in the forest crouched in a blind, waiting to spot a deer; shoveling bonobo dung; lugging great hunks of meat to the wolves; demonstrating how to field dress a rabbit. In all that time, he had never hugged her. Never put his hand on her shoulder in approval or tugged affectionately on her hair. He had never once said, "I love you."

On her good days, her mom used to say, "You know he loves you." But Raven hadn't known. And neither had her mother, drowning in her own unhappiness and despair until it drove her to leave.

Raven still remembered that day, remembered her mom saying, "Do you want to come with me?" And while her heart cried *don't leave me*, instead, Raven had shouted, "I hate you! Don't ever come back!"

She'd watched something fracture inside her mother, a fault line that couldn't ever be repaired. Instantly, she'd wanted to take it back. But she couldn't.

She'd unleashed the words, intending to hurt, to wound, and once released, they'd done their dirty work. Her mother, already unloved by Raven's father, couldn't take the dual rejection.

The next day, her mother had packed her meager belongings while Raven was at school and her father was fixing a broken fence post in Sal's enclosure. Raven had come home to an empty lodge, a paper note folded on her mother's pillow with Raven's name printed in her mother's dainty handwriting.

Her mother needed to leave before this place killed her, she wrote. She had no choice, she said over and over. The letter was full of empty apologies, line after line of *I'm sorry, I'm sorry, I'm sorry.*

Raven brought the note to her father when he returned, sweating and dirty. He'd scanned it, mouth thinning to a grim, bloodless slash. He crumpled it in his fist and dropped it on the floor, not even bothering to use the trash can.

"She was weak," he said hoarsely.

"What are we going to do?" Raven asked in a trembling voice, fighting back tears. "We have to bring her back. She has to come back."

Her father must have seen that she was devastated, that she was shattering into a thousand pieces right in front of him. But he hadn't pulled her into his arms. He hadn't hugged her. He hadn't even tried to comfort her.

Instead, his expression only hardened. "There's only one person you can depend on. Yourself."

And then he'd strode from the lodge, escaping to his wolves, leaving his daughter behind to deal with her grief the best she could.

Her father never brought up her mother again. One moment, she was there; the next moment, she wasn't. A few letters came, a few packages. Raven kept them in her room, away from her father. She knew he didn't want to see them. Raven never brought her mother up again, either.

Because she knew, deep down, that it was her fault. It wasn't her fault her mother left; it *was* her fault that she never came back.

Raven had locked up the words she wished she'd said that day somewhere deep inside her. She'd locked up a lot of other things besides. Thoughts she didn't want to think. Feelings she didn't want to feel. Tears she couldn't bear to cry.

Even surrounded by people, Raven had felt alone for most of her life. Her family had always been broken. Her parents too wrapped up in their own hurts to recognize hers. After her mother left, things only got worse.

She'd learned to stop wishing for what she couldn't have. She'd learned to stop wanting.

Now, lying here on the dirt floor of a cave, her limbs entangled with wild animals twice her size, breathing in their raw animal smell, her body warmed by their huge, furred bodies—she found herself wanting despite herself. Longing for this, right here, to never end.

She knew what this meant, what it signified for her and for them.

The wolves had made her pack.

31

S hadow woke Raven before dawn, nudging her neck with his cool, wet nose. The wolves seemed to know it was time to go.

The Headhunters would be back. And they wanted blood.

Raven had done what she could. Now it was time to run.

Her stomach rumbled. She'd been far too tired to set snares last night. She dug in her pack and tore open an instant self-heating meal pack full of some vaguely spiced faux meat that might have been chicken-flavored.

Adult wolves ate five to fourteen pounds of meat per day on average, but in the wild, sometimes twelve days or more could pass between feedings. Even as intelligent and powerful as they were, hunts were successful less than ten percent of the time. They survived on a feast-or-famine diet.

Shadow and Luna could last a few days without a meal. Still, she threw them several more strips of dried venison. Shadow gulped down his share with an eager wave of his tail. Luna growled unhappily, but she ate them.

"This time, you follow me," Raven said. She had no idea if they would. They were alphas—leaders, not followers. The thought of the wolves separating from her now, after everything, threatened to crack something deep inside her.

She couldn't do this alone.

She set the GPS destination on her SmartFlex. *Battery low* blinked back at her. Of course. Luckily, she had tucked an old-fashioned compass in the side compartment of her pack.

She shouldered her pack. Dawn was still thirty minutes away.

At least the fog had lifted. It was cold—in the forties—and the sky was clear and glittering with stars. When they entered the treeline, the leaf canopy blotted out the light.

Raven lifted her hood, drew her coat tighter around herself, and faced the thick, penetrating darkness. Her scalp prickled. She felt eyes on her. She half-expected five hundred pounds of muscle, claws, and fangs to pounce at her.

Vlad was out here somewhere. She could feel him.

For the next hour, she rode her hoverboard through the forest on its slowest setting, weaving between maple and elm and pine trees, angling sharply to avoid stumps and bushes and fallen logs. With the woods so dense, it wasn't really faster than walking, but she left no tracks.

The sun gradually rose over the treeline. Shards of golden light pierced the canopy and gilded the forest floor. The wolves ran ahead and behind her. They disappeared entirely for a while, but they came back. They always came back.

Her heart jolted at every rustle in the brush, every cracking twig. She strained her ears, listening for the rustling of the trees, the scrabble of squirrels, the chirp of a bird or fluff of its wings.

A cawing drew her attention. She looked up at a patch of sky through the trees, shielding her face with her cupped hands. Calling in raucous cries, a dozen crows soared in low circles to the northeast, just above the treeline.

In the wild, crows would follow a tiger the same way ravens followed wolves. It shifted their odds of getting fed from *if* to *when*.

Thirty minutes after the sun had risen, she found the first tracks.

She hopped off the board and knelt on the ground, crisp brown leaves crackling beneath her knees. She brushed away a few more leaves, pine needles, a spider's web.

The same deep imprint as before—thick palmar pad, four smaller digit pads.

She studied the ground. More tracks. The closely spaced indentations indicated a slow, sedate pace. The tiger had been strolling— or maybe stalking.

How long ago had he made these tracks? Hours? Minutes? They were headed the opposite direction that she was traveling, but that meant little.

Despite his impressive size, despite the burnt-orange and russet of his fur, the rich black stripes—a tiger, when he so wished, was completely invisible. He moved in absolute silence. He cloaked himself in shadows.

He would see her a hundred times before she laid eyes on him once. He could have doubled back and might be tracking them even now. Tigers were ambush hunters, masters of stealth and surprise.

She wouldn't see him until he wanted to be seen. Until it was far too late.

She slipped her pack off one shoulder and stuffed her board inside. On foot, she followed the tracks to see where they headed, whether they doubled back. If Vlad was stalking her, she needed to know.

Yellowwood, beech, and white ash trees clustered along a hilly slope ahead of her. Golden yellow spice bushes and crimson sumac were everywhere.

After about fifty feet, the tracks changed abruptly. A yard ahead of her, the dense forest broke into a clearing about forty feet wide and twice as deep. Tall grass waved in the breeze.

Just before the clearing, at the base of two poplar trees, the underbrush was matted down like a heavy log had smooshed it—or a quarter-ton of predator.

Vlad had been lying in wait for something. Or someone.

Her gut tightened. Tigers were nocturnal hunters. But if she accidentally invaded the territory of his kill, he might attack. Besides, having just escaped life-long captivity, typical tiger behavior did not apply.

Vlad was capable of anything, at any time.

Her pack grew heavy on her back. Her fingers were numb with cold. She wanted to call the wolves to her, but the thought of making a sound now filled her with trepidation.

She rose to her feet, about to high-tail it out of there when her gaze snagged on something several feet into the clearing. Something that didn't belong.

Glinting on a clutch of green mountain laurel leaves—a splash of blood.

32

Each droplet of blood was perfectly rounded, unsmudged, unsmeared. Like beads of water, only thick and dark red.

For a long moment, Raven stared at the blood, unwilling to move, her breath coming in quick, shallow pants. Her brain screamed at her to turn and flee. She didn't need to see what lay beyond those bushes.

But she did. She did need to.

She remembered Zachariah's jovial tone as he cheerfully told her, at ten, that it took less than a hundred pounds of pressure to crush a windpipe, and only five pounds of pressure to block the carotid artery. A tiger's jaws exerted a thousand pounds of pressure per square inch.

Humans were soft-skinned and thin-boned, as easy to break as a twig.

She crept closer, step by step. The horrific, grisly scene slowly revealed itself. Long red streaks in the trampled earth. A shoe, empty, turned on its side. A set of keys, shining like gold between two tree roots. A bloodied piece of khaki fabric.

And then, thirty yards into the clearing, behind a dense thicket of rhododendron, she halted. Before her lay a wide circle of horror. An arm—without a hand or a shoulder attached. Bones, gnawed white. And red, so much red. Deepest scarlet, almost black, splashed and slicked and drenched over the ground in a ten-foot radius.

The rest, her brain would not let her describe.

For several frozen moments, she stood there, stunned into silence. Her belly heaved. Everything inside her churned—her gut, her mind, her heart. She was sick, flushing hot and dizzy. Horror, shock, and revulsion flooded through her.

She turned abruptly and retched into the bushes.

She wiped her mouth with the back of her hand and retreated a step, shaking and unsteady, unwilling to turn her back on the grisly scene.

Something dark and gleaming caught her eye. A semi-automatic rifle lay in the grass, blood staining the stock, the pistol grip, the long, thin barrel. It hadn't helped the Headhunter. She tightened her grip on her own rifle.

A brown baseball cap lay less than a yard from the semi-automatic. Her stomach lurched again. She stared at the hat and swallowed the sour acid burning the back of her throat. It was the only recognizable thing left of Gomez.

He hadn't returned to the lodge with the rest. He'd stayed out in the woods, unaware that he was being hunted.

Until it was too late.

Or maybe some part of him wanted this, wanted to die quickly. He was already doomed. Over the next ten days, the Hydra virus would've ravaged his body, siphoning his life away as he transformed into a highly contagious threat to every living creature who strayed within ten feet of him.

His death might have been quick, but it hadn't been painless, or free of terror.

Gomez was a Headhunter. The enemy. He'd killed Suki. Though only because he'd had no choice, she reminded herself. He'd tried to drive the wolf away first. He'd shown mercy. Not all the Headhunters were bloodthirsty monsters.

But what did that make the ones who stood by and watched, doing nothing to stop it—like Gomez, like Damien? Whatever Gomez had or hadn't done, she couldn't help the pity and horror twisting in her gut at his fate.

Increasingly agitated, Shadow and Luna alternately growled and whined, tails curled beneath them, backs arched, jowls pulled back from their teeth. They snarled frantically, tiger musk thick in their nostrils.

They smelled death. They smelled danger.

And then she smelled it, too. She froze in mid-breath.

Raven spun, rifle up. She cocked the hammer, checked the safety. Her blood raced, panic thrumming through her veins.

In the wild, tigers would stay with their kill or bury it to return and dine over a period of several days. The tiger was still here.

The wolves knew it. They howled, whirling and lunging at phantoms. The palpable stench of his presence was nearly unbearable.

Alarm bells screamed in her head, warning of imminent danger. Her gaze flicked from tree to tree, scanning bushes, shadows, scrubby underbrush. She saw nothing. But that didn't mean he wasn't there, prowling silent as a held breath, waiting to pounce.

How many shots would she have to get off in the second or two it took for the tiger to cross thirty yards? How many bullets would it take to bring him down? Would her aim be true with a monstrous beast hurtling toward her at a fearful speed?

Most likely, she wouldn't even see it coming.

Tigers surprised victims from the side or from behind, either approaching upwind or lying in wait downwind. They rarely pressed an attack if they were seen before they'd mounted their ambush.

Shaking, she whirled, sighting more trees, more empty shadows. The forest was impossibly still. She heard no birds. Even the crows had fallen silent.

No sudden movements. What was she thinking? She knew better. Her father had taught her how to act around predators to minimize the chance of attack.

Her primitive brain was going haywire, shrieking in panic and terror, begging her to *run*.

Her primitive brain was going to get her killed.

Fleeing a tiger was all but inviting death. Inciting a chase would provoke an uncertain tiger into attacking. *Back away, step by step. Move slowly and calmly. Don't show fear.* She straightened, resisting the urge to cringe and cower, standing as tall as possible instead. It made her look like less of a helpless prey animal. Crouched down, a person appeared weaker and smaller—both increased the chances of an attack.

She remembered her father's instructions. *Stay upright. Stand tall. Look like a human.* A brave, fearless, bland and tasteless human.

Shadow stopped short fifteen feet ahead of her, a growl rising in his throat as he stared into the treeline. His hackles bristled.

The hairs on the back of her neck lifted.

A great rumbling growl thrummed through the air. It seemed to come from nowhere and everywhere at once.

Raven went rigid.

The tiger's thunderous roar slammed into her, paralyzing her muscles, constricting her heart in terror.

33

The tiger erupted out of nowhere, as though out of the earth itself. Thirty yards away, he sprang, crossing the space between them in the span of two seconds.

He launched at Raven, a blur of yellow eyes and orange fur and gleaming fangs.

A deep, primal terror surged within her. Her hands were on the rifle, but her arms no longer remembered how to lift it, her fingers had forgotten how to pull the trigger. Her heart refused to beat.

There was only time for one thought to sear through her panicked mind—she was going to die. She was going to die a hideous, painful death, and there wasn't a damn thing she could do about it.

Instead of pouncing, Vlad halted less than five feet from where she stood rooted to the earth, unable to move. Distantly, she heard the snarling wolves. Her brain registered nothing else except the lethal predator crouched before her.

The tiger, supreme predator of these woods, of anywhere. A king among kings, the undisputed emperor of his domain.

His head was as broad as a grown man's shoulders. His paws the size of pot lids. Fangs the length of a finger. Claws like meat hooks. Every inch of him radiated spectacular brute strength, power, and virility.

Ears flattened, tail lashing, Vlad glared at her with his piercing yellow eyes. Eyes hypersensitive to movement, designed to track prey. Even a full, contented cat would pounce if the prey-response was triggered.

She remained utterly motionless.

Vlad roared. It was a savage, ferocious sound. A tiger's full-throated roar was something she'd rarely experienced, and never this close. The clearing exploded with deafening noise. Loud as a jet engine and directionless, filling the space around her, expanding inside her skull, scrambling her brain, rendering her immobile.

It shook her, shook the earth, trembled through her very cells. It rumbled over and through her like an avalanche.

Think, her brain screamed at her. No one was coming in to save her but herself. He hadn't outright killed her. She had a chance, slim as spider's silk maybe, but still a chance. She wouldn't waste it.

She couldn't move, but she could speak, remind Vlad who she was.

Tigers were incredibly smart, boasting the second-largest brain of all carnivores. And they had a phenomenal memory. She knew he remembered her.

It took a supreme act of will to open her mouth, to form words on her tongue, force them out. "You know me," she croaked. "You don't want to kill me."

He snarled and bared his fangs, his tail snapping, one paw lifted. His right foreleg was streaked with blood. He was limping, wounded. Gomez must have had gotten off a shot, she realized, before the tiger tore his limbs from his body.

Vlad growled at her again, furious.

The gun. She remembered her father telling her how tigers were intelligent enough to connect gunshots—thunderous noise, a flash of pain—with the stick in the hands of a human fifty yards away.

Vlad already knew and disliked tranq guns from every single vet visit he'd ever known. Then Gomez had shot him in the leg. Vlad recognized the rifle—and knew what it was for. As long as she held it, he would view her as a threat.

Slowly, hands shaking, the tiger still crouched and snarling mere feet away, she lifted the strap of the rifle over her head. It snagged on her pack. *Damn it.* In her hurry that morning, she'd strapped on the rifle, then shouldered her pack.

Hunching slightly, terrified that her every movement would trigger Vlad into attacking, Raven shrugged off the pack and the rifle. Both fell to the ground with a thud.

Vlad roared in her face again, shaking the ground, rattling her bones.

It hadn't worked. She'd just made him angrier. Now he would pounce. Now he would sink his four-inch claws into her belly and eviscerate her within seconds—

Out of nowhere, Shadow plunged in and bit Vlad on his flank. The tiger whirled and swiped at him, claws missing the wolf's muzzle by a hair's breadth.

Shadow galloped out of harm's way. Vlad didn't chase him, but crept a step backward, hissing, still favoring his wounded paw.

The tiger's piercing eyes fixed on Raven. He was angry, defensive, but there was a weariness in his gaze, like his heart wasn't in it. Or maybe that was just what she wanted to see.

"You don't have to do this, Vlad," she said. "I know you don't really want to."

Shadow and Luna growled and snarled furiously. They spread

out, Shadow on Vlad's left, Luna on his right, with Raven directly in front of him.

The wolves darted in, snapping their jaws a few feet from his hide and springing away as he spun toward them, slashing with his claws.

His ears were laid back, his tail lashing. His eyes blazed in frustration. He kept up a continual low growl that was still loud enough to vibrate right through her, shrieking alarm signals at her brain of predator proximity and imminent death.

She forced herself to keep it together, to fight the panic. She focused on lifting her foot and taking a slow step backward. Then another. And another.

The tiger snarled and swiped at Luna. She ducked and scrambled backward, growling. He could have pounced, taking her down with a single leap, but he didn't like Shadow at his exposed back.

And he didn't want to leave his kill undefended either, she realized. The Headhunter's body lay a few yards behind Vlad. The tiger had remained in nearly the same position since the confrontation had started.

Raven took several more steps backward, until she reached the edge of the clearing. Vlad and the wolves were maybe thirty yards away. The tiger could still reach her in under two seconds if he wished.

But she was beginning to think, to hope, to pray that maybe, just maybe, he would let them live. He seemed more irritated than anything, batting at the wolves like flies, snarling at them to leave him be.

She slipped between a sugar maple and a dogwood tree, thorns snagging her pants as she stumbled backward, unwilling to take her eyes off Vlad for an instant. Shadow and Luna were both backing away slowly, backs arched, hackles bristling.

Vlad snarled half-heartedly. He hunkered down in front of his kill, protecting it.

The predators had come to a sort of understanding. Neither tiger nor wolves felt like a battle to the death this day.

She wanted to think it was because Vlad knew her, recognized her smell, associated her with affection and kindness, all those years of jerky treats, scratches and rubs against the chain-link fence.

But more likely, he just wasn't hungry. Maybe it was some of both.

Raven whistled to Shadow and Luna. "Come on!" Then she turned and fled.

She ducked and weaved between trees, around branches and thorny thickets, leaping over roots and fallen logs. Breath hissing, feet pounding, heart roaring. She ran until her stomach cramped, the pain searing her side bending her double, her throat burning. She gasped, eyes stinging, and sucked in heaving mouthfuls of precious, precious air.

The damp, earthy scent of the woods filled her nostrils. Gradually, the forest sounds returned. Sparrows, finches, and swallows chirped. A red-tailed hawk soared in the patches of sky through the leafy canopy.

The trees were on fire, exploding in shades of orange and red and yellow. Squirrels chased each other across matted clumps of dirt and leaves, the ground ribbed with gnarled, twisting roots.

She was alive. Gloriously, miraculously alive.

Shadow stalked to her side. His ears were still flattened, hackles raised. He rubbed against her side as if to make sure she was okay, to reconnect.

"We did it," she said, her throat raw, burying her hands in the thick ruff of his neck. She felt everything—the cold air chilling her skin, the wooden wing of the bird carving in her pocket digging into her thigh, the ache in her side, her chest, Shadow's fur beneath her fingers. "We faced the king of beasts and lived."

Shadow gave a low yip and bolted into the forest ahead of her. On her left, she glimpsed Luna slinking through the shadows, and then she, too, disappeared.

They would be back. She was certain of that now. She trusted them. They hadn't abandoned her to Vlad. The three of them had defended themselves—together. Together, they'd escaped the jaws of death.

She knew how lucky they were.

But she'd lost her pack. There was no way she could risk going back for it. Vlad would stay with his kill for another two or three days at least. She couldn't afford to wait for it—not with the Head-hunters hunting her, not with Ryker bent on vengeance.

If she really pushed herself, she could reach the cabin in two days. Two days of heavy exertion without food or water, unless it rained. Without her tarp or tent, without her compass. Was it even possible?

It was. It had to be.

It wouldn't be easy.

She checked her dying SmartFlex. It flickered with a sickly blue light, but it still worked. Forty-eight miles north. She could make it. With Shadow and Luna at her side, she could do this.

As she set out toward the cabin, she couldn't help feeling buoy-ant, triumphant, reveling in the flush of victory, of hope.

34

Raven hadn't hiked for more than half an hour when she heard Luna's excited yips. She stepped off the deer trail she'd been following, which meandered close to the direction she needed to go, and pushed through a thicket of sumac and mountain laurel.

She tugged a handful of plum-purple leaves and twigs aside to peer into a clearing next to a small stream. The water splashed over the rocks. A large boulder lay next to a copse of shagbark hickory trees, their shaggy bark peeling from their trunks in great swaths like wood shavings.

Luna was standing over something lying on the ground in the shadows between two trees. She bent her head, sniffing, lips curling back from her teeth eagerly, hungrily.

A calf carcass.

Alarm shot through Raven. Something was wrong. That carcass belonged in the world of the refuge, stored in the walk-in freezer of the meat house, not out here in the woods.

She sucked in a sharp breath, opening her mouth to shout a warning.

Too late. Luna stepped close and sank her jaws into the carcass, triggering the trap. A log dropped from the tree above her; the net beneath her feet snapped up, hauling her several feet off the ground.

Luna thrashed fiercely, her legs tangling in the rope. She yelped and snarled in mingled fury and fear.

Raven shrank back, crouching low behind the cluster of bushes, fighting the desire to rush into the clearing and free Luna—she still had her whittling knife in her pocket—but instinct held her back. She crouched behind a thick bush, waiting and watching.

Across the clearing, a Headhunter appeared from behind the boulder. Then another. Oman and Ryker. Their rifles were slung across their shoulders, and they both carried long, gleaming hunting knives. Wolf pelts were strung across their shoulders like capes.

Raven's lungs constricted. She recognized the distinctive markings: Titus's streaks of black. Shika's beautiful, brindled coat.

Revulsion boiled up from her gut, acid burning the back of her throat. A cold, unbearable rage seared through every part of her.

"Look what we have here!" Oman crowed. "Told you it would work."

Luna growled ferociously.

Ryker only laughed. "Knew you were good for something. Just couldn't figure out what it was before now."

Behind Ryker, Oman scowled through his thick beard, his beady eyes darkening, but he said nothing.

"Now all we need is that girl, and we can burn this damned place to the ground." Ryker prowled deeper into the clearing. The angles of his face sharpened in the dappled sunlight. He lifted his rifle and aimed at Luna.

Behind the bushes, Raven cringed, helpless and petrified and hating herself for it. What she wouldn't give for her hunting rifle. She could take out the two of them in a matter of seconds.

Her empty hands curled into fists. She didn't have a weapon worth anything. She was utterly useless.

"Not yet," Oman said, almost apologetic. Ryker swung around and glared at him. Oman shrugged. "Cerberus wants to kill this one himself. You know how he is."

Ryker sneered. "And how does he propose we bring her to him? On a leash?"

Oman pulled a tranq gun from his waistband. He shot Luna in the flank. She squealed and thrashed, but she was as helpless as Raven.

The wolf whimpered, twisting her beautiful, regal head. Her sharp eyes seemed to pierce straight through the underbrush. Luna fixed her amber gaze on Raven. Her eyes were full of confusion, fear, pain, and something else—something that looked a lot like recrimination, betrayal.

The same look her mother had given her the day Raven hurled *I hate you* at her. The day Raven had used her words like a weapon, meant to hurt, to destroy.

But she hadn't meant to hurt Luna. She'd tried to save her. Tried —and failed.

A few tense moments later, the wolf slumped, unconscious.

"You wanna bring it back alive, you do the honors," Ryker said, lip curling. He leaned lazily against an elm tree bare of leaves, arms crossed over his chest. "I sure as hell aren't lifting a finger."

He stood by and watched as Oman cut her down and tied her fore and hind paws together with rope. Oman squatted and slung the wolf's limp body over his broad shoulders with a pained grunt.

The Headhunters crashed through the forest, heading back

toward Haven. She watched them leave, the beautiful gray and brindled fur pelts on their backs rippling.

For several tortured minutes after the last sounds faded, Raven crouched there, her legs aching, her hands trembling, her pulse a roar in her ears.

They'd taken Luna. To slaughter her like a pig, to butcher her vibrant, wild beauty and reduce her to a flat, dead thing—a rug, a cape for some idiot to wear. And Raven had been forced to watch, impotent with helpless fury, utterly useless.

With the last gasp of power from her SmartFlex, she checked her GPS location. In her crippling exhaustion, the disorienting fog, and the confrontation with Vlad, she'd traveled less than four miles from Haven.

A low, despairing moan escaped her lips. She had been naive and incredibly, dangerously stupid. She had lowered her guard, letting herself believe they'd gone far enough to escape the threat of the Headhunters. Not even close.

She forced herself to stand on shaky legs.

The forest came alive with sounds—the breeze rustling the trees, the trilling of grasshoppers, birds chirping, tiny creatures creeping through dead leaves and dirt. She leaned against a pine tree to steady herself. Her hand came back sticky with sap. Blood still stained her fingernails, the creases of her palms.

She looked away.

Shadow was off scouting somewhere ahead. He didn't know Luna had been taken. How would he react when he found out? Would he understand? What would he do? Would he hate Raven, too? Blame her?

What are you going to do?

She'd watched them kill Shika, Echo, Titus. Suki. Gizmo. Who knew how many others they'd managed to slaughter last night? Was Zephyr still alive? Kodiak and Sage? Electra?

She'd stood by and done nothing. Or so little it didn't seem to matter at all.

Are you going to run?

She could. She should. She could still make it to the cabin in two days. She could survive there, alone. Wasn't that what she'd wanted all along, from the beginning?

She was a loner. A nomad. Not made for anything but an isolated, solitary life, just like her father.

It was her original plan, after all, before Zachariah died. Before her father died. Before the Headhunters came and started killing. Before she'd tried to save Haven. Before Shadow and Luna had made her part of their pack.

She sank down against the pine tree, the bark scraping her back. The earth smelled dank and slightly rotten. She shifted. Mushrooms burst beneath her hands—slick, rubbery, crumbling. Like something dead and rotting.

Do what Nakamura women do best. Leave when the going gets tough.

She was only one girl.

She'd done everything she could. She'd released the animals from their cages. She'd stalked and wounded three Headhunters, driving the rest from the woods so the animals could flee.

She'd killed Jagger.

Hadn't she already tried her best? Hadn't she done enough?

No one will blame you for running.

No one would even know. The world was dead. Everyone she'd ever cared about was dead except maybe her mom. Did she even count?

Her mother had left. Her mother ran. When things got tough, she'd taken the easy way out.

Raven drew her legs up to her chest and wrapped her arms around herself. She lowered her head to her knee and moaned. Luna was just a wolf, just a wild animal.

But that wasn't true, and she knew it, felt it in the deepest parts of herself.

Her mother had always claimed it was a mistake to ascribe human emotions to animals, especially wild animals. They were just genetics and instinct, her mother said. But she was wrong.

It wasn't *human* emotion—it was simply emotion. And some emotions—joy, anger, fear, grief—transcended species. Animals could feel, could think, could remember. They were as much sentient beings as humans. Their lives held value, connection, beauty.

Luna's life held value, connection, beauty.

What are you going to do?

If Raven did nothing, the Headhunters won.

The world outside was already destroyed, but it was the Headhunters who had destroyed Raven's world. The Headhunters who stole her home, her food, who killed the animals she cared about—the animals she loved.

What are you going to do?

To go back to the lodge now...they would torture her, kill her...

Unless...

It was ludicrous to even consider it. Insane. Dangerous.

But not impossible.

If she was smart. If she was careful.

What are you going to do?

Once, she'd planned to run, to flee, to escape her problems. But that was a lifetime ago. She was someone else now. Someone better.

She wasn't her father. She wasn't her mother. She didn't have to be either of them. She didn't have to repeat her past.

The world might have shattered into a million pieces, she might be dying of the Hydra virus—but she wasn't dead yet. She was still here.

Raven rose to her feet, steady this time.

She wasn't leaving Luna behind.

35

I t was dusk by the time Raven reached Haven again.

    She skirted the perimeter of the park outside the wrought-iron fence and crouched in the underbrush near the front of the lodge, listening and waiting. Thick dark clouds roiled across the horizon. It would storm soon.

The Headhunters were moving around, loud and boisterous and angry. At least a dozen more motorcycles were parked along the drive at the entrance. The semi-truck had arrived. It was backed up to the food storage buildings, but the bikers hadn't begun loading yet.

From what she could tell, the majority of them—twenty or so, all men—were crowded around the six picnic tables in front of the Grizzly Grill.

The men she'd wounded yesterday were hunched at one of the picnic tables, clutching bottles of bourbon they'd stolen from the restaurant's bar. They'd also found the first aid kit. Their legs were bandaged. They'd probably received stim shots, too, to keep them upright for another day or two until...until when? Were there even any hospitals left?

Right now, she didn't care. Their legs could rot off. She wished she'd had the guts to just kill them.

One picnic table was loaded with guns—mostly semi-automatic rifles, their handguns and hunting knives already holstered at their hips. They were preparing for something—a hunt.

The scent of cooking meat reached her nostrils. They were grilling. She could guess the meat.

Her stomach lurched. She forced herself to stay focused, to tamp down her rage until she could properly use it.

Raven shifted her position, creeping closer, and peeked over the top of a manicured row of bushes. She could just make out what covered the second and third tables.

More pelts, raw and stretched to dry. A bear pelt. It was facing her—she could just make out the white patch between the ears. It was—had been—Kodiak. Another wolf—she recognized Suki's dark gray fur. Scorpio wore a collection of three fox pelts across his broad shoulders, the lush red tails rippling down his back.

Anger scorched through her, turning her veins to ash. How dare they? They didn't have the *right* to steal those animals' lives, to kill them. Zoe, Zelda, and Magnus had never hurt anyone in their lives. Kodiak and Sage were giant teddy bears. And the wolves—the wolves were primal beauty and grace in motion.

They were all beautiful—and the Headhunters had slaughtered them.

She forced herself to keep her attention on the Headhunters. She used her anger to force herself to focus. She couldn't lose her edge, not now.

Cerberus held a chunk of grilled meat in his bare hands, ripping out chunks with his teeth. Juices dribbled down his chin. Scorpio laughed and took another swig of bourbon. Oman slumped at a picnic table, picking at his teeth with a twig.

Ryker wasn't eating. He wasn't smiling or laughing or swearing. He paced in a slow circle in front of the picnic tables, his movements languid and graceful.

But she saw the way he clenched his gun, the tenseness of his shoulders, the way his body was coiled, ready to spring, as alert as any predator. His eyes weren't dull and dead now; they were blazing with bloodlust.

Luna's heartbreaking, mournful howls echoed from the direction of the tiger house. The Headhunters must have locked her in Vlad's chamber.

Raven couldn't wait any longer, even though it wasn't dark yet. The Headhunters would finish eating and drinking soon. Then they'd be in the mood for hunting, for killing. They'd butcher Luna; then they'd come for her.

She traced the perimeter fence line back to the maintenance shed. Slipping inside, she strained her ears for any change in the noise coming from the picnic area. She fumbled for a lighter from the dusty top shelf, stuffed it in her cargo pocket, and wiped her grimy fingers on her pants. She grabbed the two containers of gasoline and backed out of the shed.

She ignored the meat house and made her way to the food storage building. The stench of rotting fruit burned her nostrils. She drenched the weathered wooden siding in gasoline, then peeked in the single window to make sure no one was inside before entering.

She drenched the pallets and shelves, the bags and boxes and containers full of precious, life-sustaining food. Food that could feed her for over a year. Food the Headhunters desperately wanted.

The sickening, oily stench of the gas was nearly overwhelming. A wave of dizziness flushed through her. She fought it off.

Raven backed out, splashing a trail with the last of the gasoline. She tossed the container aside and pulled the lighter out of her pocket.

Twilight was falling now, the sky rapidly darkening to indigo. Bats whirled and darted above the treeline. The first stars winked to life. The wind had picked up, carrying with it the tang of ozone. Storm clouds glowered thick and low over the horizon.

In a couple of hours, the rain would come. The storm would ensure the fire didn't spread further than it needed to.

She didn't hesitate. She lit the lighter, dropped it to the saturated grass, and leaped back.

The flames whooshed to life.

The fire raced inside, licking the walls hungrily. Almost instantly, it flared into a blaze, consuming the old wood, eating through the boards like twigs, burning through the gas-soaked interior with a startling fury.

Heat seared her face. Her eyes watered. She blinked and coughed, smoke already worming into her throat.

The air went blurry, a crackling and popping filling the air. Wood splintered and heaved. An acrid stench stung her nostrils, her eyes. The air shimmered with heat, gray with ash.

The flames surged up the dry wood, first a crackle. Fire leapt at the sky, bathing everything in a flickering orange light.

Within moments, black smoke rose in a billowing column. A signal, a warning.

Panicked shouts rose over the crackling roar.

Time to go.

36

Her heart in her throat, Raven clambered over the wrought-iron fence again and raced around the perimeter of the park, this time along the shorter side—bypassing the lodge, the restaurant, the souvenir shop, entrance and parking lot, always keeping a fringe of trees between herself and the Headhunters.

The Headhunters yelled and shouted as they ran for the blazing building, smoke spiraling into the dark sky, blotting out the stars. Their ruckus hid her own noise as she rounded the rear of the tiger enclosure, climbed over the perimeter fence, and sprinted through the overgrown grass to the tiger house.

Scenting her, Luna's whimpers and moans grew louder.

"I'm coming," Raven said. "I'm here."

The service door hung open. Raven ran inside and collapsed to her knees beside the mesh gate. Luna lay on her side, unable to rise due to the knotted ropes binding her legs. Other than the rope shackles, she seemed unharmed. She raised her head and pressed her nose against the mesh, whimpering frantically.

"I'm getting you out, I promise." Raven slapped the button to raise the sliding gate as she pulled her whittling knife from her pocket and flicked it open. Luna writhed on the cement floor, so agitated that Raven had difficulty cutting the rope without accidentally hurting the wolf.

"Hold still!" she hissed.

Luna snapped. Her jaws closed inches from Raven's wrist. Adrenaline shot through her veins. But she held her ground.

"No," Raven growled, meeting her gaze and holding it.

Luna was scared and confused. She was the alpha; she'd never needed to be submissive a day of her adult life.

"Let me help you," she said firmly.

They stared at each other for a moment—Luna's yellow eyes wild, panicked, and full of distrust, Raven fighting down her own desperate fear. She kept her eyes fixed on Luna's, willing her to understand. "We're going to have to trust each other, you and I. You're not going to bite me, and I'm not going to cut you. Understand?"

Luna's ears pricked. She whined low in her throat, her lips still peeled back, but she didn't growl. She didn't snap.

It was a good sign. Or at least, Raven chose to take it as one.

She held Luna's foreleg down with one hand, putting as much of her own weight on the wolf as she could manage, sawing at the rope with the other. She worked quickly but carefully. If she accidentally cut Luna, she'd lose whatever fragile trust they'd built between them.

She worked through the first rope. Luna tried to scramble to her feet, moaning when her hind legs collapsed. Raven pressed her down again. "Not yet. Let me work."

She paused for half a second, listening for the Headhunters. She could still hear their shouts in the distance. It was night now, the shadows inside the tiger house so deep she could barely make out Luna's pale form.

Feeling along the wolf's muscled flank and coarse fur for the rope, she moved to Luna's hind legs. She steadied herself and began to saw, the blade rasping as it sliced through the thick fibers with agonizing slowness.

"Come on, come on," she whispered. Beads of sweat gathered at her hairline. Her heart hammered against her ribs. "Almost there."

And then Luna was free. The wolf leapt to her feet and shot out of the chamber, through the service door, and out into the park.

Raven stumbled after her, blinking to readjust her eyes.

The sky was a glossy black. The bank of thunderclouds towering in the east roiled closer, closer, but for now, the moon was a bright silver against a canvas studded with stars. Everything—the trees, the buildings, the habitats, the flagstone path—was limned in a soft, pearlescent glow.

As were the three Headhunters sprinting directly toward them.

Luna stiffened, glanced back at Raven. As if to ask, *do we fight, or do we flee?*

They were maybe thirty yards away. Scorpio was shouting. Cerberus and Ryker both held rifles, Ryker's pointed at Raven, Cerberus already swinging toward Luna. Whooping and hollering, their faces hungry, drunk on blood and vengeance.

"Go!" Raven screamed. "Run!"

Luna streaked across the grounds. Cerberus fired at her.

But she was already fading away, vanishing into the mist like a white ghost.

Raven turned to flee.

She wasn't fast enough. A gunshot exploded in her ears. The bullet whizzed past her ear and struck the tiger house wall above her head with a metallic *thunk*.

"Next time, I won't miss," Ryker said.

She went rigid, her pulse thudding in her throat. Slowly, dread pooling in her gut, icing her veins, she turned and faced them.

"You burned our food stores." Scorpio scowled. His hands and face were covered in soot. "You'll regret that."

"You owe me a wolf," Cerberus growled savagely. "Not just any wolf. *That* one."

Raven lifted her chin. She said nothing.

"This little witch murdered Jagger." Ryker's long hands clenched into fists. "You kill Gomez, too?"

She refused to give them the dignity of an answer. Let them think what they wanted. Jagger's death had sealed her fate. But she'd chosen to come back for Luna. She'd made that decision herself.

"Tight-lipped, are you?" Ryker snarled.

She clenched her jaw.

Ryker sneered. "Tiger got your tongue? I can get you to talk, you know. Get you to squeal like a stuck pig."

He strode up to her, coal-black eyes blazing. She could smell his sweat, could see the pores in his skin, the knife-sharp angles of his face.

Treacherous tears burned the backs of her eyes. She blinked them back furiously. She wouldn't give him the satisfaction.

Ryker leaned in and spoke softly, his breath on her ear. "When I'm through with you, you'll be begging for your life."

Raven repressed a shudder. She raised her chin, afraid but defiant.

Ryker smiled, an ugly, dead thing. His eyes held no mercy. He punched her in the mouth.

Pain ruptured in her jaw, her lips. She tried to keep her balance, but the force of his blow knocked her to her knees.

"Little lost girl has been found." Ryker bent over her, his lip curling. "And we didn't even have to hunt her down. Shame. I was looking forward to that."

Ryker struck her again, this time across the cheek. Lights exploded across her vision. Her ears rang. Nausea clenched her gut. Dizziness washed over her in waves.

"Normally, we don't hit women," Cerberus said. He sounded very far away. "But we do make exceptions now and then."

Ryker kicked her in the stomach. She toppled, crashing backward. Cement cracked against her skull. She coughed and shuddered, gasping. She clawed at the ground, trying to rise. Pain gnawed at the edges of her mind.

Ryker delivered a savage kick to her ribs, knocking her over. Agony lanced her, slicing through her ribs like a razor-tipped spear. She licked blood from her split lip. She tried to crawl to her hands and knees.

Cerberus and Scorpio watched impassively, their faces in shadow.

Raven groaned and rolled onto her stomach. She tried again to rise. Ryker pushed her over easily, as if she were nothing more than a sack of grain. He lifted his steel-toed boot and slammed it down on her left ankle.

Something gave with a sickening crunch.

Raven writhed, groaning in agony. Her eyes stung, pain blinding her. Pain so deep and wide it engulfed her whole body. Pain without beginning, without end.

The world glimmered in and out of focus. Blackness hovered at the corners of her vision. The stars were hidden now, the sky a turbulent, churning mass of dark clouds. A gust of wind swept over her. She tasted ozone mingled with blood. The storm was coming.

Distantly, she heard footsteps.

"Is that really necessary?" Damien's voice, sharp with disgust.

"After what she did?" Scorpio scoffed. "She'll be lucky if we don't flay her—alive."

"But she's a—"

"A what?" Ryker asked, his voice dripping with derision. "A girl? Or a murderer?"

She waited, agony everywhere—her ribs burning like molten lava, her ankle throbbing, white-hot knives prying apart her bones. She clung to consciousness, waiting for Damien to say something, to defend her.

He was silent. And his silence said everything. In the end, despite his noble words, he was nothing but a coward. When it really counted, he was no better than the rest of the murderous thugs he called friends. She'd get no help from him.

She'd get no help from anyone. She had no parents. There were no police anymore. No soldiers. No one to rush in and rescue her.

An ugly, wrenching despair filled her. She was utterly and completely alone.

Her eyes burned. She didn't cry. She refused to cry, refused to give this monster an ounce of satisfaction.

Ryker leaned in close. Lightning clawed the sky above her, the pulse of white light sharpening his cheekbones to blades, hollowing his eyes to deep black pits.

He seized a handful of her hair and yanked her head up. "You killed my brother," Ryker spat. "For that, I'm going to kill you."

37

R aven awoke with a jolt.

    For an instant, she didn't know where she was, why she wasn't in bed, why she didn't hear the wolves howling outside her window and her father snoring down the hall.

And then the agony crashed into her with the force of a charging bull. With the pain came the fear—and the memories. She gasped, nearly sinking back into unconsciousness again, but the terrible memories flashing through her pain-stricken brain brought her up, up, up into the world.

Whether she wanted to be here or not.

Thunder rumbled ominously. Rain pelted the roof of the tiger house. The branches of the maple scraped against the exterior wall like fingernails.

Inside, it was almost pitch black. By the pulses of lightning flickering through the open service door, she could make out the barest outline of metal walls, the sheen of the bars in the sliding gate leading to the enclosure, the reinforced mesh of the opposite gate that opened to the square concrete box of the tiger house.

Groaning, she reached out and jerked hard on the mesh. It didn't give an inch. The Headhunters had locked her inside, caging her like an animal.

She was trapped here until they decided to kill her. Dread and panic rose within her like deep, dark waters, threatening to consume her, to swallow her whole.

They wouldn't do it quickly, or she'd already be dead. Ryker wanted her to suffer. He'd promised in the end, she would be the one begging them for death.

Outside the mesh gate, the shadows shifted, coalesced. A monstrous thing loomed, a demon, a beast.

Her lungs constricted. The room blurred. She blinked rapidly. The shadows solidified into the shape of a man.

Damien.

But no, the dark shape was too bulky, too huge. The figure leaned forward to peer at her. She caught the gleam of the whites of his eyes. She smelled smoke and the bitter, burnt stench of charred meat.

Outside, lightning streaked the sky, highlighting the hard planes of his face, the square, stubbled jaw, the twisting tattoo snaking up his thick neck, the shine of his teeth as he smiled that cruel, dangerous smile.

"It doesn't have to be this way, you know," Cerberus said.

She longed to rear up and strike him, stab him with the knife still hidden in her pocket. But the pain was too great. Everything ached. Her ankle throbbed, the sickening pain coming in pulses like a second ragged heartbeat. She licked her swollen lip and spit out the blood caked between her teeth.

Cerberus sat back against the wall outside her cage. He held a hunting knife, the long blade gleaming as he flicked it back and forth between his large hands. "I'm a reasonable man, you'll find. One of the more reasonable ones left in this world."

She tried to move. The darkness lurched. She sucked in her breath, her jaw stiff as a rusted hinge.

"When it all goes to hell, it's not the strong who survive," Cerberus continued. "It's not the prepared, not even the ones who saw it coming. It's the ones willing to do anything, to anyone, who survive. There is no moral code in the jungle. No mercy on the savanna. There are only predators and prey."

In the dark, she fumbled along her jaw, cheek, and nose with her fingers, gently pressed her ribs, wincing at the tender spots, spasms jolting through her torso.

Clenching her teeth, she tried to straighten her wounded ankle. Throbbing, fiery needles stabbed through flesh and muscle and bone. She hissed through the pain. But she could move it.

"We are going to break you in ways you cannot even imagine," Cerberus said. "The gentleman in me would rather not contemplate such a fate for you, but it is out of my hands. You killed Ryker's brother. He has the right to retribution, however he sees fit."

Cerberus paused, letting his words sink in, letting the horrors of her imagination take root, the terror digging in deep. She thought of all the ways a person could hurt and kill another.

There were other species who killed their own kind, in battles for dominance, territory, the right to mate.

When Raven was seven, before Gizmo and Zephyr and the other bonobos, the refuge took in several chimps. Six months later, two of the chimps conspired to assassinate their alpha. They waited until Zachariah and the other keepers had gone for the night, then attacked, biting off their target's fingers and testicles and leaving him to bleed to death.

The next morning, Raven had discovered the dead chimp when

she went with her father to clean out their night house. She still remembered the damp chill of horror, the way her father had stepped back with an involuntary gasp, his face closing like a door.

Her father had liked to believe animals were elevated, special, above the horrors and atrocities of humankind. And maybe for the most part, they were. But not always. Animals weren't free of the stigma of brutality. They were as capable of cruelty as anyone.

In the wild, groups of chimps waged war on other troops, hunting, terrorizing, and murdering their adversaries, several holding down an enemy while others dismembered him. When male lions joined a new pride, they killed the cubs sired by another lion. Juvenile foxes, owls, and hyenas sometimes killed and ate their siblings. Dolphins and orangutans were capable of rape; orcas, of sadistically killing for entertainment.

But only humans had turned the murder of other humans into an art form—en masse, by the hundreds of millions, by the billions. Terrorists had just destroyed the world with the Hydra virus, intentionally annihilating their own kind. At the intimate, personal level, one man butchered another for greed, jealousy, power, or for no other reason than perverse pleasure, because they could.

"There is an alternative," Cerberus said softly, "if you will consider it."

Thunder crashed. The rain pounded harder. She swallowed and stared blindly up at the ceiling until her vision blurred. She was thirsty, parched, her mouth caked with sand. She hadn't had anything to drink since that morning.

The tense silence grew thick between them. He was waiting for her to respond. He was going to make her speak. This was a game to him, like a cat toying with a mouse before it settles down to the business of dinner. The way wolves ran a bison to exhaustion, wearing down its hope, its desperate will to live, step by despairing step.

She should ignore him. She shouldn't give him anything, not even her words. If it was her fate to die, she was determined to do it on her own terms.

But with every minute that ticked away, with every precious, painful breath, her resolve eroded. Hope, after all, was the very last thing to let go. Even in the face of catastrophe, of a devastating apocalypse, of utter despair, it held on.

The wind shrieked around the tiger house, beating the maple's branches against the wall. Thunder boomed and crashed. It felt like nature itself was screaming its outrage.

Finally, she croaked, "What is it?"

Cerberus grunted as he shifted against the cement wall. The razor edge of the knife glittered. "The white wolf. You came back for him. A few of the men say they saw you with both of them in the woods. You know where they go."

She thought of the den Luna had led her to, of the night sleeping between the wolves, the steady heat of them, the coarseness of their fur pressed against her skin, the dank, wild smell filling her nostrils. The awe and wonder and beauty of it.

"You can take me to the white wolf."

She closed her eyes. Dread settled like a stone in her stomach. "You want the pelt."

"Those wolves are like nothing I've ever seen. Like mods...but not. The white one is...marvelous. He's the alpha, there's no doubt. I'm an alpha. He's an alpha." She could feel him grinning in the dark. His eyes shone greedily. "We're meant for each other."

"Luna *is* an alpha," she said with a grim, terrible satisfaction. "But *he* is a she."

Cerberus was silent.

"Wolf packs are families. The alphas are paired, male and female. In some ways, the female makes more decisions than the male. She chooses who to hunt, picks a specific prey animal out of the herd. She tells the other wolves when and where to strike."

"Enough!" Cerberus snorted dismissively and rose to his feet. "Enough nonsense." His gaze raked over her, lingering on her face. His lip curled. "There is a place for you in the world that remains. You are quite the specimen. Beneath the dirt and that ugly scowl, your delicate Asian features could serve you well. You could be taught to be a proper woman. *If* you learn to hold that tongue and respect those empowered to rule over you."

"Go to hell," she whispered between split lips.

He laughed mirthlessly. "If you bring me to the white wolf, I will spare your life. If you do not, I'll allow Ryker do as he wishes with you."

"You're lying."

His expression went cold. He raised his voice over the crash of thunder. "I am a man of my word. If I say it's going to happen, then it will. You've been watching us these last few days, I presume. Then you know my men respect me. They will obey me, whether they like it or not."

She couldn't find the wolves, not for certain. But she had an idea where they might be. Besides, the wolves would come to her. She knew they would. They trusted her. They'd made her pack.

Cerberus sheathed the knife. His shadow loomed over her, blocking out everything else. "Decide now."

She felt her powerlessness like a crushing weight, insurmountable, hopeless. But beneath her despair, a steady thrum like a heartbeat, an insistence, an urgency, a fierce will to live. *I will survive this. I will survive this. I will survive this.*

Instinct, as ingrained within her as any wild animal. That desperate impulse for self-preservation above all else, above honor and goodness and even love.

Damien was right, after all. Her father was right. Humans would do anything to survive.

Life or death. Death or life.

It was her only choice. Her only chance. She stared bleakly at the darkness above her. Consuming, absolute.

"I'll do it."

He turned for the door, the pouring rain. "We leave before dawn."

38

The storm raged for hours. In a single night, most of the leaves were shorn from the trees. Early the next morning, the clouds were still thick, the sky a gray bowl of ashes. The air was cold and brittle.

Raven tasted the wild tang of ozone on her tongue. The storm wasn't finished yet.

She hobbled between Damien and Cerberus, with Ryker right behind her. Scorpio, Oman, and a few others took up the rear. Her hands were bound in front of her with zip ties. The men all carried semi-automatics, their expressions grim.

They hacked their way through the dense undergrowth, thorns raking at their legs and arms, cursing as their clothing snagged on thickets of thorns, their clumsy feet tripping over roots.

Rain began to fall, heavy and full, splatting on the branches, the matted ground, streaming in rivulets from the bushes. In minutes, they were soaked, clothing sodden, boots sloshing through damp mud.

The wind howled and shrieked through the empty trees, rattling the bare branches. Pine needles glistened. The tree trunks gleamed darkly. Deep in the forest, the air was rank with moisture and decaying leaves, thick with the promise of winter.

They'd been hiking for almost two hours. Raven's wet pants clung to her body, but her arms and torso beneath her jacket were dry—still freezing, but dry. She lifted her head and drank the rain, soothing her parched throat.

"Hurry up," Ryker growled, prodding the small of her back so hard she stumbled over a tree root worming across her path. Pain stabbed her left ankle. Damien tightened his grip on her arm, holding her up.

Cerberus had injected her with one of the adrenaline stims from their med kit. It dulled the pain, sharpened her senses, and kept her on her feet, with Damien's help.

She hated his nearness, hated how she needed him to walk, hated how he kept shooting her tense, heavy glances, his brows knitted, his eyes full of shadows.

"You okay?" he whispered between gritted teeth.

Raven ignored him. She had nothing to say.

"I know, stupid question."

They trudged through the wet and the gray, heads ducked against the rain. Cerberus marched on ahead, twisting to stare back at her for a moment. "Tell me when to turn," he growled darkly.

Rain sluiced off her hood. Her skin was chilled, clammy. The raw, unrelenting wind scraped her hair back from her face, pummeling her already sore body. But her misery was nothing compared to the dread and horror tangling in iron knots in her gut, nothing compared with the darkness howling inside her heart.

"You shouldn't have come back," Damien said softly, low enough that only she could hear beneath the blur of the rain. "You were free."

"I don't expect you to understand," she said. Guilt dug into her ribs. "I couldn't just leave her."

"I tried to do something." He looked at her, eyes bleak. "It wasn't enough."

"No," she said. "It wasn't."

She glanced at him. Rain trickled down his narrow face, plastered his russet hair to his scalp, beaded on the silver ring piercing his lip. His features were as cunning, as sharply handsome as she remembered. But his expression was solemn, pensive.

"Why didn't you turn me in, back at the lodge?"

"You were brave," he said after a moment. "I...maybe I admire that."

She said nothing. There was nothing to say. Her bravery wouldn't help her now. It was too late for that.

She stumbled; Damien caught her. His hands were strong. His nearness was strangely comforting. He wouldn't save her, but at least he was here. It was something.

"Move faster," Ryker hissed behind them.

She pushed away the pain in her ankle, focusing on reading the signs of the forest. A gnarled trunk of an oak with knots in the shape of a triangle. An outcropping of rock beside a spruce with its top half sheared off.

A paw-print here and there, almost—but not quite—smeared by the rain. Mostly hare, raccoon, badger, and deer tracks. But a few others. She noted bent and broken twigs, a torn spider's web, a crushed leaf, a snarl of her own black hair snagged on a bramble.

She had no SmartFlex now, no GPS to guide her, but her father had taught her how to find her bearings in the middle of the woods, how to track the creatures of the forest—even if that creature was herself.

Scorpio hunched inside his coat, dark and glowering, his head bent against the wind and rain. "How much longer?"

"This is a waste of time," Ryker growled. "Just give me the girl and we'll be done with this mess."

"We're done when I say we're done," Cerberus said, his voice sharp with warning. Scorpio and Ryker fell silent.

They reached a steep incline. Raven shuffled past the stump of a great oak as tall as her shoulder, the broken off bits jutting like teeth. On her right, a cluster of boulders. Rhododendron bushes creaked in the wind.

She stepped into the clearing and lifted her head. The sky was dark, chaotic, turbulent clouds churning overhead. The rain splattered her face, soaked her hair.

"What are you doing?" Ryker stepped into the clearing behind her, his face darkening. "If you've tricked us, so help me—"

"We're here," Raven said.

She whistled. One long note, two short ones.

39

"The white wolf's den is here," Raven said. "Across the clearing."

The Headhunters entered the clearing. They spread out, rifles up, scanning the ground, the trees. Thunder groaned. Lightning splintered the sky.

The keys were still there beneath the large rhododendron bush in the center of the clearing. They glinted like a treasure, the rain washing away the dirt and leaves. Gomez's sodden baseball cap lay crumpled beside them, brown as dirt, barely visible through the sheets of gray rain.

And there, a few yards from the bush—her pack on its side, the hoverboard still sticking out of the top.

It was a huge risk, bringing the Headhunters here. But she didn't know what else to do. She wouldn't betray the wolves. She refused to give them Luna or Shadow. It might have saved her life, but that wasn't the life she wanted to live.

It was a desperate move—a rash, reckless, foolhardy choice in a very short list of options, each more terrible than the last. There was only one chance to get out of this alive, both for Raven and the wolves.

If it didn't work, at least she would die on her own terms. And the wolves would be free.

Would Vlad spare her a second time? She believed he would. She had to believe. She was betting everything on it.

She strained her ears, even knowing she wouldn't hear him. Fresh adrenaline shot through her veins as her gaze swept the tree-line. There was nothing to see.

There wouldn't be. Not until he was ready to attack.

"I didn't want this to happen," Damien said in a low voice. He'd remained beside her at the edge of the clearing. "What Ryker did to you..."

"You stood there and watched."

"There was nothing I could do."

"Is that what you tell yourself?" But there was no venom in her words, no blame. Not anymore. She understood now the feeling of being trapped between two impossible choices, each with terrible consequences. In his own way, Damien had found himself trapped, surviving but caught in a life he hadn't chosen to live.

She saw guilt swimming in his eyes. Remorse.

"Maybe you're right," he said.

She shook her head, blinked water from her eyes. "I can't expect you to sacrifice your life for me, a stranger." Survival was about more than keeping yourself breathing. It was about choices and sacrifices, choosing what you could live with, and what you couldn't. Everyone had to make that decision for themselves. "You helped me twice. More than I could ask for. Thank you."

He looked at her, startled. "You're welcome."

"Over here!" Scorpio called, his voice shaking. He stood behind the rhododendron bush. He'd found the body.

Ryker, Cerberus, and Oman followed him. Ryker and Cerberus swore. Oman stumbled back, his face going ashen beneath his beard. He turned and retched.

"So that's what happened to Gomez," Ryker said coldly.

"Those damn wolves tore him to pieces," Cerberus said, both in horror and awe.

Raven clenched her jaw and said nothing.

The Headhunters milled around the wide circle of the kill. "Here's an arm," Scorpio said hoarsely. He almost sounded afraid. If he wasn't now, hopefully he would be soon.

Raven eyed her backpack. Twenty yards, if that. She would have to run straight across the clearing, grab the pack, and head for the opposite treeline. Once she got a bit of a head start, she'd jump on the hoverboard and escape without leaving any further tracks.

She yanked her arms, the bindings digging tight and painful into her wrists. It wouldn't be easy to get to her knife with her hands bound. And she'd be hobbling across the clearing—not running. Her jerky, fumbling movements would trigger Vlad's prey response.

Unless he was otherwise engaged.

Cerberus and Ryker strode toward her. Cerberus's face contorted in rage. Ryker's black, flinty eyes shone with triumph—and anticipation.

"Bring her here!" Cerberus ordered.

Damien tensed beside her. "I'm sorry."

"It's okay," she said. "I understand."

Damien's jaw pulsed. He tightened his grip on her arm and led her deeper into the clearing. "You don't have to do this," he said to Ryker in a low voice.

Ryker snorted. "You going soft on us, boy?"

"There's no shame in sparing her—"

Ryker shot him a contemptuous look. "Shut the hell up and give her to me."

Damien hesitated. He grimaced, dread and fear flashing in his eyes, and she saw how every word he spoke cost him something. "And if I don't?"

Ryker sneered. "How about I gut you both together? That what you want?"

"Watch yourself, Ryker." Cerberus's voice went cold and hard. "Damien, give him the girl."

Damien hesitated, his expression taut, sharp eyes flickering between Cerberus and Raven. His piercings glinted as lightning streaked the sky. "I don't think—"

"Damien!" Cerberus growled.

Without waiting for Damien's response, Ryker sprang forward and shoved Damien aside. Damien went sprawling, landing hard on his backside in the wet grass.

In one fluid movement, Ryker unsheathed his hunting knife, grabbed the back of Raven's head, and pressed the blade to her throat. "Now," he hissed in her ear, "where were we?"

"Where's the den?" Cerberus asked her. He barely glanced at Damien, who was pulling himself to his feet, scraping the mud from his pant legs. "I'm only going to ask you once."

Raven swallowed, the knife jabbing deep. "It's here, just through the trees—"

Ryker's eyes narrowed, shiny-dark as beetle shells. "Liar."

"I told you what would happen if you played me." Cerberus's tone was flat, but his eyes flashed with anger. He nodded at Ryker. "She's all yours. Get it over with."

Ryker gave her an empty smile, full of sharp white teeth. He was going to enjoy killing her. She could see it in the menacing gleam of his eyes, his lips parted in expectation, the thrill of it contorting his lean, knife-edged features.

Damien stood silent, muddy and rain-slicked, his gaze anguished. But he did nothing. He said nothing. Raven was on her own.

Lightning lit the underbelly of the clouds, streaking across the sky. Torrents of rain poured down. Wind roared over the clearing, bending the grass sideways, creaking through the trees, clawing at her with cold, frantic fingers.

She'd miscalculated. Vlad wasn't here. For whatever reason, he'd abandoned his kill early and moved on to greener pastures.

It was over. She'd gambled and lost.

Cerberus swore. "For the last time, where is the damned wolf?"

She blinked the water from her eyes and raised her chin in bold defiance. She was going to die, but she hadn't given them everything. They hadn't won. She'd made sure of that. "The wolves aren't here and never were. They got away. You'll never find them. You failed."

Cerberus lunged at her, enraged, but Ryker seized her hair and dragged her against him. She couldn't help it. She screamed. She tried to wrench free, but the knife blade bit into her throat, drawing blood.

At least she was in the woods when death came for her. At least she would die with rain and wind on her face, grass and dirt beneath her feet, the mouth of the sky swallowing her up.

At least—

Out of the corner of her eye, she saw it.

A streak of motion bolted into the clearing. Then another. One white, one black. Twin demons of growling, snarling fury.

40

R aven swallowed a horrified scream as the great black wolf launched himself at Cerberus.

Almost simultaneously, the second wolf, white as pure driven snow, slightly smaller but no less ferocious, charged Ryker.

The clearing exploded in shouts of confusion and fear.

Luna sprang at Ryker. She lunged, closing her powerful jaws around Ryker's forearm. Ryker fell back from the force of the blow, shrieking as the wolf's teeth sank into flesh, muscle, bone.

Raven stumbled with him, entangled in his flailing limbs, dragged to the ground. The knife was wrenched from her neck. A line of fire seared her throat. She rolled in the wet grass and managed to clamber to her hands and knees.

"No!" Raven screamed. "Run! You're supposed to run!"

The wolves were supposed to be far, far away, running safe and free and alive. They weren't supposed to come back here. They weren't supposed to save her.

Scorpio and Oman ran toward Ryker, who was on the ground,

Luna atop him. They screamed and shouted, their rifles drawn but unable to shoot for fear of hitting the Headhunter.

Ten yards away, Cerberus managed to slam the butt of his rifle against Shadow's muzzle. Shadow let out a pained whimper and darted out of harm's way. Three other Headhunters armed with semi-automatics were sprinting toward them.

Run! Raven's brain screamed. This was her chance. But she couldn't run, she couldn't leave the wolves in the hands of the Headhunters, not when they had come back for her, had put themselves in harm's way.

The wolves had made her pack. They'd made her family.

She had to *do* something. She had to help them.

Time slowed. Raven felt every frantic beat of her heart, every ragged breath. She crawled in the slick, wet grass, desperately searching for Ryker's long, serrated hunting knife.

Rain pelted her exposed head. Frigid water dripped down her neck, sliding cold, seeking fingers beneath her jacket. The world was gray and unrecognizable, blurred by the raindrops clinging to her eyelashes.

There. A glint of steel.

She seized the knife in both hands and reared up on her knees. She scanned the chaos of the clearing. Shadow was holding his own against Cerberus, springing in and galloping aside, leaping and snarling and biting.

Cerberus fired several times but couldn't aim fast enough. Shadow was a black ghost, dissolving in the rain, untouched, before reappearing to plunge in and tear a gash in Cerberus's arm, snatch a bite from his leg.

Only a few yards away, Ryker wrestled Luna. He was still on his back, Luna crouched over him, snarling and snapping.

Scorpio and Oman circled them both, firing warning shots with their rifles. Luna ignored them in her single-minded pursuit. She was ferocious, unrelenting, determined to down her prey.

Ryker managed to wrench free from Luna's jaws. He cradled his left arm close to his chest, his jacket sleeve shredded, the flesh beneath pulpy and leaking dark red blood.

The smell was faint, so faint it took her an instant to recognize it. The hairs on the back of Raven's neck stood on end. It was unmistakable—the sickly-sweet smell of buttered popcorn.

Hope surged through her.

"Luna!" she shouted.

With his right hand, Ryker jerked his handgun from its holster and punched at Luna's face and muzzle as she repeatedly lunged for his throat.

Ryker twisted the gun and fired.

Raven screamed.

She staggered to her feet and took a step toward him, knife handle slipping in her trembling, rain-soaked fingers. Her ankle buckled. Pain speared up her leg. She stumbled, forced herself back up.

Thunder boomed overhead, cracking the sky into jagged pieces.

Ryker fired again.

Luna slumped across his chest.

"Get up!" Raven cried. "Get up!"

Luna's muscled, sinewy body twitched, her great chest heaving once, twice. Her regal head sagged as she let out a single low moan and went still. The rain pelted the wolf's thick white fur.

Luna was dead.

Raven sank to her knees, bereft. No cry escaped her lips. She was silent, her pain and grief clenched tight as a fist inside her.

She watched in numb disbelief as Ryker shoved the dead wolf

off himself and clambered to his feet. He kicked the limp body savagely, mercilessly, again and again, cursing.

Raven felt flayed, every nerve ending exposed. A sick terror filled her. She was falling, falling, falling into a chasm with no bottom.

"Stop," she whispered in a strangled voice. "Stop it."

Ryker heard her. He spun, rain sluicing down his sharp face. He clenched and unclenched the fingers of his tattered left arm. His eyes glinted. Rage contorted his features—rage and scorn and a twisted, sadistic anticipation. "You."

The roar was loud as a great crack of thunder, trembling the ground beneath their feet.

Raven had no time to think, to feel, to form anything but a single distraught thought—*tiger*.

41

The tiger exploded from the underbrush. He launched at the Headhunters in a ferocious orange blur, flying twenty feet in a single bound, spanning the distance between himself and his prey in under two seconds. An air-born, arcing missile of death.

Oman spun and fired a burst of several shots. But in his panic, the gun veered wildly. He had no time to correct his aim. The tiger was on him.

Vlad collided with his target at full speed, claws extended, jaws gaping. Man and beast went down together.

The tiger raised his sledgehammer paw and struck Oman in the side of the head. The man's skull snapped back. The blow might have broken his neck. There was no way to know, for in an instant Vlad plunged his fangs into the Headhunter's throat and crushed his jugular.

Oman writhed, gurgling, struggling to breathe, eyes rolling wildly. Black-red lifeblood gushed into the wet grass.

His face twisted, an ugly, guttural gasp spitting out, blood bubbling from his lips. For a moment, he clawed weakly at the tiger's furred chest, then went suddenly limp.

Everyone in the clearing froze, shocked, terrified, awe-struck. Even Shadow stiffened, turning toward the new, more dangerous threat.

Vlad cut an astonishing figure, awful in his enormous size and power, a quarter ton of coiled muscle and sinew. In the rain, the burnt orange of his coat was even more brilliant, the shaggy white fur of his chest and belly shining, the bands striping his broad back a rich, oily black.

Vlad stood over Oman's body, his muscular shoulders rippling, his every movement imbued with stunning grace and terrible beauty. He still favored his bloody paw, but it had hardly hampered him.

His yellow eyes narrowed to slits, his ears flattened against his skull. He bared his fangs, every one of his four-inch claws unsheathed, razor-sharp.

"Shoot him!" Ryker cried, raising his rifle.

No sooner had he spoken than Vlad swung his great head, his gaze riveted on Ryker. It happened with a terrible, slow-motion vividness.

With a snarl of fury, Vlad sprang.

Airborne, he arced fifteen feet through the rain.

Cerberus was closest, he had the best vantage point, the best chance at taking the shot. Maybe he was frozen in fear, or maybe he chose to do nothing, to watch—whatever the reason, he did not pull the trigger.

The tiger pounced on Ryker. He slashed the man in the face with a savage swipe of his claws, knocked him to the ground, seized his head in his enormous jaws, and shook him like a rag doll.

There was a terrible wrenching sound, a sickening crunch of bone caving in on itself. Vlad shattered Ryker's skull.

The tiger crouched over the dying man, tail lashing, back arched as he roared, great head swinging back and forth, ready and seeking his next prey.

As long as it was a Headhunter with a gun, Raven could still escape. Luna was gone, but Shadow wasn't. Raven wasn't.

And then she saw it. In the frantic blur of the attack, in the gray of the rain and the chaos of the clearing, she'd missed it. Vlad was slobbering. He was bloody from the kill, but this was something else —something *wrong*. His jowls dripped with red-streaked foam. The fur of his chest and forelegs was matted with it.

He stared straight at Raven with fixed yellow eyes, pupils slitted, unblinking. His jaws hung weirdly, hinging open and closed, almost as if he had no control over it.

The realization jolted through her. Vlad had consumed Gomez's diseased flesh.

Vlad was infected.

He was no longer himself. The virus had infiltrated his body, his mind, taking command. His diseased brain sought to bite and infect everything within sight.

And she was his next target.

Five hundred pounds of apex predator sprang at Raven.

42

The world stopped. Rain droplets froze in midair. The chaos of screaming and shouting went dim, as if Raven were trapped underwater. Everything went blurry—everything except the tiger.

Vlad surged toward her, a streak of orange and black fury. She had three seconds, if she was lucky. She raised the knife—how useless it was, how little it would do—and whistled. One long note. Two short ones.

Ten feet from her, powerful hind legs already crouched for a final spring, the tiger hesitated.

Did he recognize her whistle? Deep in his diseased predator's brain, did some part of him remember an affinity for a vulnerable human? Whatever the reason, he paused.

And in that liquid, suspended moment, Cerberus shot him.

The bullet struck Vlad's hindquarters. With a roar of pained outrage, the tiger spun and hurled himself at Cerberus instead.

Raven couldn't waste a second. This was what she'd planned for, the distraction she so desperately needed. She started to run.

"Shadow!" she screamed. "Go!"

Shadow had abandoned his attack on Cerberus and now stood over Luna's body, nudging her neck with his muzzle and whining softly.

Raven staggered in the slick grass, waved her bound hands at him. "Go!"

He flicked his ears toward her. He shook his head, as if coming out of a fugue. He seemed to understand what she meant, what she was asking him to do, because he bolted across the clearing.

Shadow raced past her backpack, dodged the boulders, then paused between the trees, looking back over his shoulder. Waiting for her.

She fixed her gaze on her pack and hobbled toward it, pushing out everything else—Vlad's roars, the shouts and howls of the Head-hunters, the blasts of the guns. She sucked in her breath with every stab of pain in her ankle. She stumbled, drenching her pant legs, smears of mud crusting her legs, rain pelting her face.

Ryker's hunting knife slipped from her fingers. She scrambled for it for a frantic second, searching in the long grass. There was no time. She had to go.

She dragged herself to her feet, wincing.

Behind her echoed the roars and screams and gunshots. She hobbled faster. She had maybe a minute to escape, if she was lucky.

She tripped over a rock she should've seen and went down hard, barely getting her arms in front of her to protect her face. Her body struck wet ground, squelching as she struggled in the muddied grass. Spasms of pain ripped through her ribs, her ankle. Her vision went blurry.

Someone seized her arm and yanked her to her feet.

Terror spiked through her. She reared back, about to head-butt him, rip out a chunk of his cheek with her teeth, whatever she needed to do—

"Raven!" Damien cried. His face was ashen, his eyes wide and horror-stricken. "Let me help you!"

She nodded, too numb and terrified to argue. "My pack. The gun."

He leaned down, seized the straps in one hand, and hauled it to his shoulder. He slipped the rifle strap over her shoulder and across her chest. With his other hand, he took her elbow and helped her shuffle haltingly to the edge of the clearing.

Damien paused several feet inside the treeline. He shot a nervous look across the clearing. She followed his gaze.

Cerberus, Scorpio, and several others were backing Vlad against a boulder. Vlad was snarling, ears laid flat, back arched. Blood-flecked foam dribbled from his jaws. His hindleg and left foreleg both hung uselessly, his flank matted with great streaks of scarlet.

Vlad attempted a lunge. Cerberus and Scorpio fired at his paws, driving him back. Vlad howled, his right foreleg collapsing beneath him.

Raven stopped breathing, waiting for the kill shot. It didn't come.

The Headhunters laughed and jeered. They were shooting at the tiger's legs on purpose. Injuring him, but not killing him. They were torturing him.

Vlad screamed in agony. Guilt ripped through her. She'd done this. She'd brought the Headhunters to Vlad. She tried to tell herself she'd had no choice—but she *had* made the choice. The choice to risk Vlad's life to save hers, Shadow's, and Luna's.

She had hoped the tiger would take the Headhunters by surprise, attacking a few of them while she escaped. She'd hoped Vlad would escape too, vanishing deep into the forest.

She'd never wanted him to die, to suffer. But she had still taken that risk.

She hadn't known he was already infected. That knowledge didn't ease her guilt, her grief. She had loved that tiger, and now he was dying.

"Your hands," Damien said, forcing her back into the moment. She couldn't do anything to help Vlad now. If she didn't hurry, his death would be for nothing.

She held out her bound wrists. "Can you do something about this?"

"I don't have a knife—"

"In my pocket. My whittling knife."

Damien shoved his hand deep into her cargo pocket and pulled out the knife. She stiffened, ignoring the water dripping from his hair onto her neck, the feel of his fingers sliding against her hip, the closeness of him.

He sliced through her bindings in a few quick, powerful strokes. She gestured for her pack and he helped slide it over her shoulders. He pulled out her hoverboard and handed it to her.

She activated it with trembling fingers. Her whole body was shaking.

"Here." Damien pulled something out of his pocket. An auto-injector in a plastic sleeve. He ripped off the plastic. "Cerberus told me to bring an extra stim in case yours wore off and you passed out on us. It'll buy you a few more hours. That's all I can give you."

She nodded gratefully as he yanked up her sleeve and injected it into her left arm. "Thank—thank you."

A gunshot exploded. Then another. Vlad roared in pain and rage.

Raven flinched.

She met Damien's gaze. Rain plastered his hair to his forehead and dripped down his face. It softened his features. He was still sharply handsome, all hard angles, but he looked younger, almost vulnerable.

She felt a pull, deep inside her. He had tried to do the right thing in spite of his circumstances. He could have just looked out for himself. He should have, but he didn't.

She was still alive because of him. She said the words before she could let herself stop them. "Come with us."

The briefest of smiles creased his mouth—grim, but genuine. It brightened his whole face. Then it darkened, a sad twist to his lips. "Thank you, but no, I can't."

"You aren't like them. You don't belong with them."

He shook his head, his mouth pressed into a thin line. His gaze darted toward the clearing again. "I owe Cerberus my life. I can't just—"

"Yes, you can."

"He's family. He protected me."

"You're afraid."

He blinked. "Maybe. Yes."

"Come anyway."

His jaw tightened. "There's no time. You need to go. Where are you headed? North?"

For a second, she hesitated, her instinct to lie, to protect herself. But this boy had just saved her—again. He wasn't the enemy. He was a friend. Someone she could trust. Needed to trust. She nodded mutely.

"I'll tell them you went a different direction. I'll cover for you." His eyes darkened, flashing with something she couldn't quite read —doubt, regret, longing. "That's the best I can do."

Another gunshot. Vlad gave a horrible, deep-throated whimper. Raven longed to clap her hands over her ears to shut out the awful sounds, to sink to her knees in the mud in grief for this magnificent creature as he died.

But she couldn't. She couldn't spare a moment, a second, for Vlad—or for Luna. Not now.

Deeper in the woods, Shadow whined impatiently.

It wouldn't be long before Cerberus turned his attention back to her, seeking revenge for the death of his men. He was a man of his word. She didn't doubt he would hunt her down if he could find her.

She had to make sure he didn't find her. Or Shadow. Not ever.

Vlad let out another agonized whimper.

"Will you give him mercy?" she asked. "Please."

"I will," Damien promised.

"You should leave them," she said. "When you're strong enough, brave enough."

The muscle in his cheek jumped. "Maybe someday I will."

Raven grasped Damien's hand—his palm warm and rough against her own, despite the rain. His fingers tightened over hers.

For a moment, they were connected, sparks of electricity shooting up her arm, fizzing in her belly. For a moment, she longed to hold on, to never let go.

He'd made his choice. And she'd made hers.

She pulled away, climbed onto her hoverboard, and fled for her life.

43

For the next night and day, Raven and Shadow fled. They did not stop to eat. They did not stop to drink. They ran on, and on, and on, terror and grief chasing at their heels.

She did not think of the cabin. She did not think of Haven. She did not think of her father or the animals, alive and dead. She shut it all out of her mind before the weight of it crushed her.

She thought only of escape, of staying alive for one more minute, one more hour, one more day.

The thunder stopped, the rain ceased, the towering storm clouds rolled back. But the sky remained stubbornly dark and gray, as if the heavens were in mourning with them.

She rode her hoverboard for hours and hours, every muscle in her body aching and bruised. Shadow ran with her, loping a few dozen yards ahead or behind, disappearing for an hour or more, patrolling, scouting, always alert for danger.

The woods were grim and dark and wild. Stinging branches slapped her face. The air was dense and close. She felt it like an expelled breath on the back of her neck.

She was hopelessly lost. But still, she kept going.

Sometime near twilight, Shadow appeared and halted ten yards in front of her. She tilted back her right heel to halt the board. "What is it, boy?"

His tail drooped, his head bent. He'd looked like that since Luna's death—depressed, grieving.

He whined and loped off through the trees to the west, a right turn from the direction they'd been headed for the last sixteen hours. The shadows were deepening as night fell. She could hardly see him anymore.

He did his over-the-shoulder look, beckoning her to follow. She did.

After about half a mile, he led her to a tiny clearing in the center of a ring of spruce trees. A sheer rock face towered about forty feet above her head. A narrow crevice opened at its base, leading to a small cave just large enough for them both.

Her throat thickened. Somehow, Shadow seemed to sense that she needed this.

Suddenly, she was so tired she could barely stand. Every muscle in her body ached. The adrenaline stim had worn off hours ago. Her face was one big bruise. Her ribs were burning, her ankle a throb of white-hot pain.

"Thank you," she whispered.

She stepped off her hoverboard, grimacing from the jolt of pain, and glanced at the power meter. It needed sunlight to charge. Though it was night—cicadas and crickets bursting into song, stars glinting overhead—she hoped to sleep for at least twelve hours, well past dawn. She left the board outside the cave beneath an open patch of sky.

Raven lowered herself to her hands and knees and crawled inside, her left ankle dragging.

Shadow did not come with her.

"Shadow!" she called.

She waited. But he didn't come.

She crawled back out, unwilling to be alone. Not tonight.

Shadow stood on a shallow outcropping a few yards away. He threw his head back toward the sky, raised his muzzle, and howled.

It was a haunting, mournful sound, filled with sorrow, clear and pure as a bow drawn across a violin.

It was a requiem. An elegy. A howl of grief for the lost pack member who wasn't ever coming back.

He howled for his lifemate, for Luna.

Raven listened. And as she listened, she felt her heart cracking open. She felt all the pieces of herself falling away, shriveling to nothing, revealing the raw, pulsing center deep within her.

All the grief and sorrow and pain she'd been burying so deep since her father died—no, since long before then. Since her mother left, abandoning her.

Since the day she first realized her father couldn't love her like other fathers could. Since she was five, the first time she remembered feeling completely alone, and believed she deserved to feel that way.

She let the pain flow through her, a dark river of sorrow drowning her from the inside. She grieved for Zachariah. She grieved for her father. No matter whether he was the father she'd wanted, he was the father she had. And she loved him.

She grieved for her mother, for the love she'd stifled with bitterness and resentment, locking it in a place deep down. She hadn't realized what she'd done, how much she'd lost, until it was too late.

She grieved for Gizmo and Kodiak, for Shika, Titus, and sweet Suki. For Vlad, who didn't deserve the death he'd been given. And for Luna—a wolf, an animal, a different species—who'd still made her pack, and then proved her devotion by sacrificing her life to save Raven's.

The world had been broken for a long time. But now it was shattered, the remaining shards sharp with cruelty, suffering, loss. It felt empty, forsaken. Bleak and hopeless.

But within the suffering, the loss, she felt the connection—silvery, thin as a spider's web, but strong as steel—threaded between herself and the wolf howling his sorrow into the sky.

Her eyes burned. Tears gathered at the corners of her eyes.

For the first time in three years, she let them fall.

And finally, she wept.

Later that night, Raven crawled inside the cave and collapsed on the rocky ground, exhausted and weary, emptied out. Shadow stood over her in the darkness and nuzzled her neck. She held out her hand to him. He flopped down beside her, his flank pressed against her side.

"It's you and me, now," she said softly.

He whined, gazing at her with those beautiful, mournful eyes.

"I can't do this alone, okay? I need you. We need each other."

She buried her hands in the scruff of his neck. She nestled her cheek against his fur and breathed in his scent—of earth and bark, grass and wind, of all things wild and primal, of fierce creatures prowling through deep, dark woods, of love and pack and family.

44

R aven and Shadow traveled mostly at dawn and dusk, sleeping in the woods by day. Sometimes she set up her tent and sleeping bag, a few times Shadow found them another cave, or a shelf of rock to shelter beneath.

Each night, Shadow howled his sorrow and grief. Each night, Raven wept with him.

As they traveled, she kept roughly parallel to the river, tracking north with her compass and using her Lifestraw to filter the water for drinking. She foraged for food, gathering fallen hazelnuts, hickory nuts, and black walnuts to boil later. In spring and summer, she could forage for highbush blueberries, elderberries and sawtooth blackberries, wild sweet potato and wild ginger roots, cattails and clover, and of course, dandelions. The entire plant—flower, leaves, and roots—was edible, if a bit bitter.

Her father had taken her on numerous camping, hiking, and hunting trips to the cabin. Each visit, he'd make her memorize each edible plant and then find it again on her own the following trip. "You can't depend on anyone but yourself," he'd said.

Her heart ached at the memory. In some ways, he had been right. But in other ways, he was wrong.

Because of the things he'd taught her, she could survive. But she didn't just want to survive. She wanted to live. She understood the difference now.

Isolation wasn't the answer. It couldn't be. Not for her, not anymore.

Gradually, the pain in her jaw, ribs, and foot lessened. Her swollen lip healed. The ugly yellowish-green bruises marring her ribs faded. She could walk instead of hobble, but her ankle refused to heal properly. She wasn't sure if it was broken, fractured, if ligaments were torn, but she kept her boot on at all times to act as a supportive splint for her ankle.

Ryker's cruelty had left her with a limp and a constant dull ache that radiated from her ankle down to her toes and up her shin.

But she was alive. And he wasn't.

While Shadow dozed in the afternoons, she set her snares, searching carefully until she found a well-used trail leading to a rabbit burrow. After three days of empty snares, she finally caught dinner.

She skinned and dressed the rabbit, then roasted it. She built a fire the way her father taught her. The first time, she worried that she wouldn't remember. But she did. She remembered everything with an ache in her chest and grief stinging the back of her throat, so strong it nearly took her breath away.

She crouched over the small ball of tinder she'd gathered, mostly dried moss and pine needles, and struck the flint with the edge of the steel with a glancing motion, gently fanning the sparks into a tiny flame.

Earlier in the day, she'd dug two holes, each eight inches across, a couple of feet deep. She made a tunnel between the two at the base to connect them and filled one with twigs, bark, and small sticks.

The second hole acted as a chimney to suck oxygen down to feed the fire. The fire was nearly smokeless, and the flames couldn't be seen from afar.

She didn't doubt there were others like the Headhunters out there. She had to remain vigilant at all times.

While she waited for a snare to catch a squirrel or rabbit to roast, she whittled, carving little birds, wolves, bears, and a tiger. She'd forgotten how much she loved the feel of the wood beneath her fingers, the shape of something hidden within, just waiting for her to bring it out into the open, fully formed.

She'd let her resentment take something precious from her. Her carvings, and her memories of her mother and father both. But not anymore. She held onto every memory—the good and the bad. They were all she had left.

She left the wooden figures on stumps, in nooks between branches, nestled in the hollow of a tree. Maybe someone would find them. Maybe it would make them smile, give them a tiny sliver of hope. Sometimes that was enough to keep going, to keep trying.

One night, the woods echoed with a series of howls far off in the distance. For a second, she hoped it was Loki or Aspen, but there were too many of them. A few wild wolf packs survived further north in the Chattahoochee National Forest. They wouldn't normally travel so near humans, but everything had changed.

There were far fewer humans now.

Shadow pricked his ears. She waited to see if he would howl back. Sometimes a pack would announce a vacancy, putting out a call to any lone wolves who wished to fill it. Potential candidates would be challenged by the pack to ensure the chosen one was strong enough, smart enough, capable enough to defend and protect his new family.

Did Shadow feel like a lone wolf? Did he want to find his own kind? He gave her a mournful look, his amber eyes steady as he stared at her.

"Do you want to go?" she asked, her throat tight.

He gave a low yip in the back of his throat. His tail swished once, twice, three times.

"It's okay." The words hurt to speak them. But she knew love always gave a choice. "You can go if you want to."

Shadow stayed.

Another piece of her heart fit back together.

Two days later, just as dawn was breaking, they crested a hill and came upon an outcropping overlooking a small town. The sky glowered a bleary gray, the morning air chilly.

Shadow hung back, wary, but Raven hadn't seen a town since the pharmacy at Clay Creek. "Five minutes," she promised. She wanted a paper map to help her get where she needed to go. Also, she was intensely curious.

Shadow whined unhappily, but gave in and loped after her.

A street sign welcomed visitors to Mayfield, home of the state's best fried okra. There were a few stores, a gas station, a tiny hotel, and several smaller roads lined with clusters of small, hunched houses.

It was eerily quiet. There was no movement, no life.

As she got closer, her stomach knotted in apprehension. This town was worse than empty. It had been ransacked, looted, turned inside out.

Trash, crumpled leaves, broken glass, and scattered papers littered the sidewalks. The roads were pitted and pocked with potholes, the parking lots weed-infested and riddled with cracks.

Hundreds of abandoned, gutted cars blocked the road. Most sported broken windows, their interiors scraped clean of anything but trash. The gas station's windows were shattered. As was the barber shop and hardware store. Small holes punctured the walls and riddled the driver's side of a Jeep parked in front of the gas station.

Shards of glass thrust from the frame of the gas station's broken front door. Inside, deep shadows crouched in every corner. She blinked to adjust to the dim light.

The shelves were mostly picked clean. Several racks were tipped over. The air smelled foul, like rancid milk and foul, rotting meat. Flies buzzed.

There were no paper maps to be found. She didn't know what she'd expected. Everything was electronic now. She could've gotten the information she needed in five seconds on her SmartFlex. But without the net, without electricity, all that knowledge was gone, erased in a few short devastating weeks.

She left the gas station and passed a sagging hotel, a dusty SUV parked in front of the drive. A putrid stench filled her nostrils—something decomposing, rotting. Her hand covering her mouth and nose, she peered through the window.

Two men slumped in the front seats, rust-brown blood staining the masks still over their mouths, blood leaking from their eyes. The bodies were bloated and discolored, their swollen limbs locked in rigid agony.

She stepped back fast, breathing hard. This was how her father had died. How ninety-five percent of the world had died. Probably her mother, too, though she didn't know for sure.

As for Raven, she hadn't suffered so much as a cough since Zachariah had splattered infected blood in her face. That was over two weeks ago.

There was only one reason she wasn't already dead.

Raven was immune.

But the knowledge offered little comfort. Her immunity couldn't save her father or Zachariah. It hadn't done a damn thing to save Luna or Vlad or any of the others.

And it wasn't only the Hydra virus that made this town dangerous. It was the people. All towns were dangerous now. And cities.

From now on, they'd skirt the towns and highways, stick to the safety of the woods. But she needed a plan. She needed a destination.

Raven turned away from the town. "Let's go," she said to Shadow.

They left together, the wolf loping at her side.

45

L ater in the morning, as they were making their way back through the woods, Raven heard voices. She jumped off her hoverboard and hid behind an oak, rifle tight in her hands.

A child's voice rang out. Raven stiffened in surprise.

Shadow's hackles raised. He pressed his muzzle to her side before trotting out of sight, vanishing into the trees.

Raven remained hidden as three figures strode closer, crashing noisily through the underbrush like a herd of elephants. She peeked around the edge of the trunk.

There were two boys and a girl. The oldest boy and girl both looked about Raven's age. The girl was Filipina, short and plump, maybe seventeen or eighteen, with thick black hair to her shoulders and choppy bangs.

The little boy looked about eight, also Filipino and likely the girl's brother, with big black-button eyes in his brown face and a thicket of unruly hair that stood up all over his head.

The older boy was African-American and huge, with broad

shoulders, a barrel chest, and tree-trunk arms and thighs. He looked intimidating, until he smiled at the little boy, his warm eyes crinkling, his smile both kind and mischievous.

They wore hiking backpacks, a sleek black handgun holstered at the girl's hip.

The older sister was holding the little boy's hand, but he was giggling and trying to escape and grab the older boy's hand instead. "Nice try, Benjie," she said, exasperated. "You think I'm letting go of you for even a second? You have to stay right with me so I can keep you safe."

But the little boy—Benjie—pushed between them and grasped the older boy's hand, which was so large the kid's entire hand disappeared inside it. He looked up adoringly at the big guy. "I can hold both your hands at the same time, right, Finn?"

"Always the negotiator." The girl rolled her eyes good-naturedly. "What do you need to remember?"

"Stay together, stay safe," the little boy repeated, his face solemn.

"Got it," the girl said.

As they trudged past Raven's hiding spot, the guy and girl both holding the boy's hands as they pushed through thickets and trampled dead leaves, the sister smiled down at her brother, love and affection shining in her eyes.

Raven watched them go, straining to hear long after they'd passed out of sight. She remembered her mother's birthday letter. *Find a good group of people you can trust. Don't be alone, Raven.*

It was a risk. People were a risk. Trusting was a risk.

There were plenty of bad people. There were only a few good ones.

She thought of Zachariah. Damien. Her parents.

She knew now her father had done the best he could, in his own way. The war had broken an already reticent man into something that couldn't be put back together.

But he hadn't run. He'd stayed, and he'd struggled through his own brokenness to give her the best gift he knew how to give—the knowledge to survive.

Her mother had been wrong to leave. Or at least, to leave and never come back. But Raven couldn't hate her either. In the end, her mother had risked everything to leave her own sanctuary to rescue her daughter. She hadn't made it, but that didn't lessen her sacrifice.

And in that loss, Raven found her forgiveness.

The world was ugly. But the world had always been ugly. Like always, you took what you were given and you made it your own. She looked at Shadow, felt love and hope and determination rising up within her.

She knew the truth now. Those few good ones made the difference between isolation and connection, between survival and living, between death and life.

Raven was going to find her mother.

But first, she was going to find out if these were people she could trust.

The End

ACKNOWLEDGMENTS

Thank you to my awesome beta readers. Your thoughtful critiques and enthusiasm are invaluable, as always: Lauren Nikkel, Michelle Browne, Kimberley Tremblay, Jessica Burland, Sally Shupe, Lia Riccio, Jeremy Steinkraus, and Barry and Derise Marden.

To Michelle Browne for being a great developmental and line editor. And to Eliza Enriquez for catching those last little proofreading errors. You both make my words shine.

To my husband, who always helps with deadlines and plot holes and listens patiently to problems about imaginary people.

And to my kids, who I love more than anything. You are my everything.

ABOUT THE AUTHOR

Kyla Stone is an emerging author of contemporary young adult fiction and suspense/dystopian novels. She lives in Atlanta, Georgia with her husband, two children, and two spoiled cats. When she's not writing or spending time with her family, she loves to read, hike, draw, travel, and play games. Her favorite food is dark chocolate.

Kyla loves to hear from her readers. For news and new releases, visit her at:

www.FaceBook.com/KylaStoneBooks

www.Amazon.com/author/KylaStone

Email her at KylaStone@yahoo.com

SNEAK PEEK OF RISING STORM: THE LAST SANCTUARY BOOK ONE

Terror coiled in the pit of eighteen-year-old Amelia Black's stomach. Sweat beaded her forehead. The fabric of her dress clung damp and chilly against her skin.

The polished marble corridor stretched ahead of her, silent and empty but for the bodies.

In just a matter of minutes, the whole world had fallen to pieces.

It was hard to believe that only a few hours ago, the *Grand Voyager* was a glittering jewel of crystal and glass, a lavish fulfillment of every wish and desire, a shimmering promise of dreams come true.

But it was all a lie. This wasn't a dream; it was a nightmare. And with the nightmare came the terror, the shrieking and running, the beautiful bodies falling, limp as dolls.

Now, there was nowhere to run. Nowhere to hide.

Amelia strained for any sound over the crashing thunder of the storm. She crouched behind the counter of a coffee bar along the corridor of Deck Ten of the *Grand Voyager* luxury liner.

The display cases were all smashed, glass shards littering the marble floor. A humanoid service bot slumped against a bank of storage cabinets, smoke hissing from the bullet hole drilled into its forehead. Above the sink, the broken holoscreen flickered.

The voices came again. Two or three of them, from somewhere down the corridor.

She didn't know who they were. Terrorists, pirates, hired thugs, or private militia. It didn't matter. They were ruthless killers. And they were hunting her.

Because of her father, the powerful leader of the Coalition. Because of what he'd done.

If they found her, she was dead. They would use her as a bargaining chip, a pawn to get whatever they wanted from her father. They'd torture her. Then, they'd kill her.

But she was sick of being a pawn. She'd die rather than give in. She had her own plan, if she could live that long.

She'd thought the terrorists were the deadliest threat on this ship. She was wrong.

Thunder crashed. Waves rocked the ship. The floor tilted, and she stumbled, glass fragments jabbing into her bare feet. She sucked in her breath. She had to ignore the pain, the mind-numbing fear. She had to *think*.

Her family was still out there, trapped somewhere on the ship. Her brother, Silas. Her mother. And Gabriel. She winced. She couldn't think about him. Not now.

She'd done something, too. Something she couldn't take back.

Lightning shattered the night sky through the floor-to-ceiling windows on the far side of the corridor. Rain lashed the glass. The awful rat-a-tat of gunfire exploded from somewhere above her.

The voices grew louder. They'd be on her in thirty seconds or less.

Her heart leapt into her throat. She was cornered. Trapped. Out of time.

If you enjoyed this sneak peek of *Rising Storm*, you'll love *The Last Sanctuary* series. Find it at your favorite online retailer.

Made in the USA
Coppell, TX
14 June 2022

78825339R00166